A Drift Out of Time

Also by Bruce Macfarlane

Science Fiction

Out of Time

A House Out of Time

The Space Between Time

The Time Palace of Mars

The Time Travel Diaries Trilogy

Short Stories

The Webs of Time

The Butterfly Effect

An Audio script for the Time Travel Diaries

History

Notes on Arthurian Literature

A Drift Out of Time

The Second Book

from

The Time Travel Diaries of

James Urquhart and Elizabeth Bicester

by

Bruce Macfarlane

2nd Edition

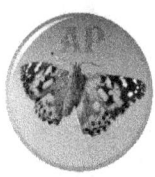

Aldwick Publishing

A Drift Out of Time

This is a work of fiction. Names, characters, places, and incidents are either the product of the author's imagination or are used fictitiously.

Copyright © 2018 Bruce Macfarlane
Aldwick Publishing
www.aldwickpublishing.com
All rights reserved..

ISBN-978-1-9164024-2-3

DEDICATION

To my wife, Julia

A Drift Out of Time

Preface

"In the summer, on baking hot sky-blue afternoons, the cliffs of the chalk white Severn Sisters are crowded with holiday makers picnicking and enjoying the view.

What's not apparent to most of them is that if they could climb down the face of Seaford Head a little and press themselves against the chalk, they would disappear through the wall and enjoy a more fantastic view of the remains of a Martian invasion force."

Book II of the humorous and sometimes romantic Time Travel Diaries of James Urquhart, science lecturer and sometime rambler, living in 2015 and Elizabeth Bicester, Victorian Cambridge graduate, whom he met at a cricket match at Hamgreen in 1873.

A Drift Out of Time

Contents

A Drift Out of Time

Acknowledgements

Editing: Julia Macfarlane

Images & Illustrations.

Art work by author using PicsArt Photo Studio for
Android

A Drift Out of Time

Introduction

After stopping a Martian invasion of Earth and ruining the Weber Institute plan to take over the world, James and Elizabeth have returned home for a bit of peace and quiet to find they are not only in a different future but a different aspect of themselves.

Moreover, the Martians are still trying to colonise Earth after their failed invasion and Marco Batalia, the Director of ComsMesh, is loose in time trying to reconnect the interplanetary dark net to help them.

In their quest to get back to their own world James and Elizabeth travel back and forth between Mars and Earth and find themselves drifting across time and space through different pasts and futures until eventually they find a home; and in the process discover who the Martians really are.

Fairies will never look the same again.

$$--- \sim ---$$

A Drift Out of Time

Prologue

Weber Institute, Mons Olympus, Mars.
Comms Intercepts: Marco Batalia;
Classification: Rogue.
Time-Space World-Line: 23 Earthside

Incept 2021a.12.1.15

I am stranded here with knowledge of a future that does not exist. The closure of the Time Servers at Midhurst by Urquhart and Bicester has altered time and provoked a premature invasion by the Martians who expected Earth to be subservient and locked into ComsMesh. The Martians' defeat by germ warfare was catastrophic leaving the landscape littered with a substantial part of their military force.

I have also learnt that Rollinson has obtained and read the Bicester and Urquhart diaries and drawn the conclusion that by the aid of my time machine at Midhurst I was complicit in the server shutdown. He has informed the other Weber directors of his suspicions. I am to be summoned to the Board tomorrow.

Incept 2021a 12.1.20

No one believes me. I am to be relieved of my duties on the Board of the Institute and assigned to SocRehab and sent to Mars. My only hope is to get back to the past, restart the servers and warn Mars of the germ defence. But that requires a time machine. I need to find the diaries to see if there is any help there.

Last night I went to Rollinson's lab to look for the diaries. The chest was on top of a filing cabinet in his office. I undid the clasp, opened it and took out the two diaries. But as I retrieved them I noticed a thin rectangular copper plate at the bottom. I put the diaries on his desk and returned to the box. I moved my fingers around the plate and found an indentation which allowed me to lift it revealing a black circular disc about eight inches in diameter. I removed it carefully out of the box. There were strange markings around the edge. I do not remember Urquhart talking about it but there must be a reason it was there. I decided to take it. So as not to arouse suspicion I replaced the diaries in the box, and after closing the lid left with the disc.

Incept 2021a 12.1.22

I am back home after another meeting. There is a guard outside my door. I am to be sent to SocRehab tomorrow for assessment before being sent to Mars.

This black disc. What is it? Is it connected to the diaries? I need to find out its function. To my knowledge Rollinson has not reported it missing and might not even know of its existence. Time is running out. I must examine it.

I have found a device of seemingly Martian design which gives access to a network which is not connected to this world. After many trials I managed to access it. It works by thought. I am in the Dark Net. I looked for Bicester and Urquhart and discovered their diary records which show that they were given a Time Transponder by a science fantasy writer H.G. Wells. This transponder was used by them three times after they closed down the Time Servers at Midhurst and records that by aid of its use they effectively caused the defeat of the Martian invasion of Earth. They then inexplicably vanished.

Incept 2021a 12.1.26

I have located the Urquharts in the Dark Net. They are in a close but different time line. Somehow Wells' transponder has access to a fifth dimension that allows the user to slide across time bands. The fact that the Dark Net is able to see other futures as well suggests it may be possible to travel in and across these bands.

I am left with two options.

The first is to return and restart the Time Servers and retrieve my time machine so I can prevent the shutdown.

The second is to somehow find a way to leap across to the Urquharts' time path and trap them in time.

They are coming for me. I must think, think! Time is running out.

Weber Institute, Mons Olympus

Report on the disappearance of M. Batalia.

Report 2023a 36.7.15

SocRehab arrived at Batalia's residence at 0400. Finding no answer, the door was forced and entry to his apartment made. There was no trace of him. The guards reported he had arrived at about 17:00 the previous evening and not left after that. Staff stationed outside on the road of his building and at the rear did not see him leave.

A Time Transponder was found at the residence. It recorded Batalia last location 2016 Midhurst, Earthside.

--- ~ ---

A Drift Out of Time

Part I

Round and Round the Garden

A Drift Out of Time

Chapter One

E.

I opened my eyes expecting some new adventure. Instead I found we had returned to James' attic. The relief made me almost faint. I turned to him. He looked shattered. No doubt I did not look much better. We held each other tight for some time in silence.

But then as I drew away I noticed by the faint glow from a fanlight there was something different. The dark screens and James' extraordinary armchair had vanished. Instead an old desk and a broken Windsor chair stood in the corner covered in dust. Damp strips of distemper now hung from the walls and rafters and I could hear the wind blowing through the eaves.

I looked at James and he saw my face.

"What's happened?"

"I do not know. Where or when are we James? This seems to be your attic but it is not the one we left."

He turned around and immediately stared at where his machines had been.

"I don't understand. Where's all my gear? This room looks like it hasn't been touched for years. God! How long have we been away this time? I think we better get some light."

He went to the door where in his time a small handle was normally found to illuminate a room.

"There's no switch. I'm sure it was by the door. Damn! We must still be in Wells' time! How did that happen?... Just a minute. Don't move. I can hear something."

He was right. Someone was coming up the stairs to the attic. If we were really in the 1890s who lived here? Was it an ancestor of James? And if so what would we say?

--- ~ ---

J.

I stood looking at the door. I could feel Elizabeth's warm breath behind me on my neck. As the footsteps got closer on the stairs her hand gripped my arm. Desperately I tried to think of excuses for being in a stranger's attic but none were forthcoming.

What was Wells really up to? He had sent us home but he seemed to have left us in his time!

Then the footsteps stopped. The handle turned and the door slowly opened and what looked like a woman's head appeared silhouetted by the landing light. She moved further into the room then our eyes met. I recognised her immediately. It was my sister Jill! What was she doing here?

"Jim! God you gave me a shock. I thought it was rats. What are you doing in the attic and who's that with you? .. Oh, Elizabeth! Hello again. How the devil did Jim entice you up here? I think you'll find he normally keeps his etchings in the back bedroom."

I was about to return her banter when in the weak light from the landing I noticed there was something that was not quite right about her. She was wearing a grey suit cut rather like those worn in the 40s and her hair seemed to have lost its usual soft bounce. Even her make-up seemed a little too obvious which was certainly not like Jill who prided herself on her 'natural' looks. I replied a little uncertainly.

"Hi, Jill. Er... it's so good to see you again. We've just been back to the 1890s saving the world."

"Yes", said Elizabeth joining in, "and we met Mr Wells again who was kind enough to send us back here. Though I do not know how."

"I see. So you found the attic was another time portal. What made you think of that?"

She said it as though it was an unusual place to be. Jill usually referred to it as my 'shed' where it was often suggested, quite unfairly I might add, that I spent too much time playing with my toys. I was beginning to wonder whether we were actually back in 2015 or some time else? And if some time else what was Jill doing here? I decided to try a little test.

"It was just an idea to try the attic. By the way, Jill, where are all my computers? You haven't sold them, have you?"

She looked at me rather perplexed then said "Computers? Do you mean your ready reckoners and slide rules you're always playing with? They're in the bureau downstairs."

This was worrying. What year were we really in? Were we back in the 50s or 60s? But if we were, how did Jill get here? I tried again hoping the shock of meeting us again had caused her to misunderstand what I had said.

"No, I mean my computers and monitors and all my electronics?"

"I'm sorry, Jim. I really don't know what you're talking about. Is he OK, Elizabeth?"

I could tell Elizabeth sensed a difference as well. They had become quite close during Elizabeth's stay here and both had come to depend on each other in their journeys to each other's time.

"He is as well as can be expected, Jill, after our fight with the Martians. I trust they have not returned."

"OK, OK. You've both lost me completely now. I don't really... Just a minute. Why are standing in the dark? Are you hiding from someone?"

"I couldn't find the light switch."

She looked even more perplexed.

"You've picked up some strange phrases, Jim, while you've been away. The lamplighter's over there."

And she walked over to the wall and pressed a metal button. There was a slight hissing sound and what I took to be a gas lamp lit up.

I bit my tongue and squeezed Elizabeth's hand in the hope she would say nothing and said, "You're right, Jill, we've had some strange experiences and we're just about knackered, to say the least. Can we go down and have a cup of tea? It might restore our senses."

___～___

E.

The living room was familiar but had different aspects to those I remembered. The patterned walls had been replaced by a cream painted, embossed paper and instead of the rows and cabinets of books there was just one shelf of moth-eaten novels and magazines. A patterned rug, that might have been woven by someone who had once seen an Axminster from a distance, covered the centre of the floor on which were two comfortable chairs and an old settee. As I looked around trying not to appear too surprised I sensed that there was something missing. It was so obvious I didn't see it at first. Then I noticed. The large black screen that normally occupied half a wall had disappeared and had been replaced by what I took to be a rather faded print of Constable's 'Haywain'. James' Pre-Raphaelite copies were nowhere to be seen. I began to understand what was worrying James.

But before I could comment Jill came back into the room with a large tray of tea and biscuits. We sat down on the sofa and managed to engage in small talk for a while which I hoped deflected our concerns. Then after a cup of refreshing Indian tea I turned to Jill and said as nonchalantly as possible:

"So, how long have we been away this time?"

"Oh, about two days. I left you after that rather nice dinner you gave me. You didn't mention you were planning another trip. I would have liked to have come."

I was about to enquire as to how she had occupied her time when James took his phone from his pocket. He was always playing with it and no doubt on this occasion had removed it by unconscious habit. Jill noticed it too. Usually she took the opportunity to make a humorous comment about his addiction to its operation, with which at times I must admit I agreed, and would normally join in at James' expense but instead she said.

"What's that, Jim?"

I gave James an expression which I hoped he understood. He did.

"Oh err... it's a case I picked up. It might be from a phonograph."

"Can I have a look?" She turned to me. "He's always picking up bits of junk, Elizabeth. But I expect you know that already."

"I must admit that James does find and accumulate the most extraordinary items and displays an acute interest in them that would have passed by us lesser mortals."

11

"You never know when some of these things might come in useful." said James.

"On occasion this is true, James, and sometimes I am singularly impressed that after retreating to your 'hide-away' with a new found toy you will emerge after a short while holding a refurbished contraption that until then I had not realised we needed."

I must admit that I have often noticed married men create an alternative 'nest' to their home, to which they 'disappear' for short periods to recuperate from the travails of family life, while their wives address any difficulties in the matrimonial home that arose and contributed to their absence. Some men have such a place in a quiet corner of the family abode, others in a small summerhouse at the end of the garden and a few elect for a small allotment at a distance that requires the family to take an omnibus to reach them. Luckily James was, in general, approachable and available in his attic for the smallest assistance. I complemented James on this on one occasion to which he replied that much depended on a wife's skill in timing the request to ensure a good response, not to mention taking into account any limitations he might have in dealing with the request. I felt it prudent not to mention that I have found if one approaches a subject in the right way a man can be persuaded to carry out a request which up to then he had thought was beyond his limitations. But this small skill must be used sparingly if it is to be effective.

However, I digress again. If I'm not careful James will wonder what I am doing with all his ink.

Jill was still examining James' phone and with more interest than I expected. She held it in her hand and turned it over. The screen was black and thankfully she had avoided touching the buttons.

"Does it do anything?"

"Not that I can figure out." Said James in as naturally careless a voice as possible.

After a little further examination, she handed it back.

"Well, Jim, no doubt it will find its way into that drawer of yours with all your other bric-a-brac. Anyway, I'd better get some shopping in now that you're back. Need anything apart from the customary bottle of wine?"

"No thanks. Oh, could you pick up the local paper?"

"I'll try. They've usually all gone by now. Help yourself to some more tea and biscuits; they are in the cupboard".

After she left James turned to me.

"God, Elizabeth, look at this house! Gas lamps everywhere and gas heating as well. No sign of a telly or radio. Do you think they've invented electricity?"

As I looked around trying to comprehend what this future was I noticed something familiar to me.

"Isn't that a telephone, James?"

"Ah! Yes. It's an antique I picked up in London. Never got round to connecting it up properly. Just used to crackle when I tried it."

He walked over to it and lifted up what I took to be the speaker and half-jokingly said into it. "Hello! Anybody out there who can tell me when we are?"

We nearly jumped out of our skins as a familiar voice emanated from a small oval grille.

"Hello, Mr Urquhart and also hello, Miss Bicester, I presume you are there as well?"

With all my strength I composed myself and replied.

"Yes, Mr Wells, and by the bye I am now Mrs Urquhart."

"Are you? I forgot. So many time lines to remember."

I have to admit I was a getting little bit disappointed with Mr Wells' appearances. They always seemed to bring trouble of sorts.

--- ~ ---

J.

I was beginning to suspect we had been cast into a sea of time and Wells was the fisherman. But what was more disconcerting was the fact that the telephone was not connected to any wires. I tried to remember when and where I bought it. But first I needed to know what was going on and why did Wells keep on appearing just at the right time?

"OK, Wells, I don't know what you're playing at but let's start with when and where we are and also what is this telephone?"

"I will answer the easy question first, Mr Urquhart. You bought it from me in that second-hand shop in Charing Cross Road about a year before you met Miss Bicester. Do you remember?"

That's why he looked familiar when we saw him in the cavern at Midhurst!

"God, yes! I remember. It was like something out of a Steampunk picture. I should have realised such stuff never really existed. Except then of course time travel was just a figment of my imagination. So, the difficult question, where and when are we, Wells?"

"You are back in 2015 but in a world where poor Mr Maxwell did not publish his paper on electromagnetism. Hence, as you may have discovered, you are living in a world in which chemistry rules."

"What, no electricity?"

"Oh, there is electricity. There are many electrical machines, even computational machines; much of industry is powered by electricity, but for lighting and heating people have stayed with coal gas."

"But what about Mr Edison and his light bulb?"

"He was imprisoned for what he did to that elephant."

Elizabeth turned to me.

"What elephant, James?"

"Don't ask. So Wells, the country is run on coal. Pollution must be terrible."

"No, Mr Urquhart. The apothecaries have done a wonderful job capturing the waste products and CO_2. It is a pity they weren't allowed to apply their skills in your world, or should I say the world you think you should be in."

That was scary.

"What do you mean? What world do you think I'm supposed to be in?"

"You broke from your world when you bought that telephone, Mr Urquhart."

--- ~ ---

E.

Wells' last comment was extremely disconcerting as it took me back to when I first met James at the Cricket Club. He had thought that was his first time travel. Yet later we discovered he had already met my cousin Henry and was not aware of it. Did this mean there was more than one James out of time? If this was true, then there was more than one of me!

This is most distressing. I am beginning to doubt who I really am. Am I the person I think I am? Is James the same James I met at Hamgreen and Helmsley? Have I lost the James I first fell in love with? I must find out but first we

15

had to ascertain what Mr Wells was doing. I gentle prised the device out of James' hand and put the voice box to my lips.

"Mr Wells, as you know we asked to go home but like a devious fairy or Genie you have given only what we asked for and no more."

"There was no more I could give you."

"But you knew we wished to return to our own time again!"

"What time is that, Mrs Urquhart? Do you think you travel along one line of time? Each time you travel there are a number of opportunities. The further you deviate the lower its probability of exact replication. Thus on each arrival, so far luckily, you have arrived at a place which is mostly familiar. But you may find yourself one day completely out of time in a place in which your previous existence is not even a memory."

"I think I understand that, Mr Wells, but when I travel is it really just me who travels or is there a myriad of paths each with a copy of James and me? What I mean by that is at this moment in time are there hundreds or thousands of us?"

"That is well put, Mrs Urquhart. The answer is yes, but not that many. Only certain futures exist. By that I mean only those that are possible."

We both stood still, silently looking at each other trying to absorb the implication of this reply. I tried to think of all those other Elizabeths. I imagined a set of adjacent rooms like the one we occupied now stretching to infinity and in each room there were James and I but slightly different and the further away from this room the more different we and the rooms and the world became. This thought reminded me of when I was a child. My mother had a dressing table with a mirror to which were attached two hinged mirrored wings which allowed observation of one's complete visage. But by turning them at right angles and looking left and right I could see dozens of little Elizabeths alternately looking towards and away from me.

But before I could follow this fantasy further Mr Wells made a shocking suggestion. "Are you with child, Mrs Urquhart?"

I instantly looked down at my skirts and then at James. I could see he was quite taken aback by this as well.

I replied, "No, I am not, Mr Wells! Nor is it of your concern!" For I was not a little angry at this enquiry into our private affairs.

James was immediately supportive in his own way.

"That was a bit uncalled for, Wells. Not to mention rather bloody rude!"

"But it is of concern, "said Mr Wells, "Because in at least one other time line Mrs Urquhart returns pregnant."

I sat down and starred up at James. Thoughts of carrying a child now lost flooded my emotional senses. This aroused intense maternal feelings which I had not known existed in me. I felt angry that somewhere was our child which I might never see.

James took the device from my hand.

"Christ, Wells! Were you out to lunch when they taught what made women tick when you were at school?"

"I apologise to Mrs Urquhart. I was only trying to reinforce what I was saying with an example."

"Well, try not using what we are or what we might have been in other lives as an example. We simple humans don't want to know. Jesus!"

James turned to me and held both my hands. They were shaking a little. "Are you alright, Elizabeth? I really feel for you."

James' understanding of what I had not said but felt was a great comfort and restored me to some semblance of normality, but my emotions were in turmoil. I steadied myself. I was in this world and this was the only world with which we had to understand. I took the device back and said. "Mr Wells? This is really too much. We are here now. Pray tell me what we are to do now in this world?"

"That is for you to decide. I suggest you look for Mr Batalia."

And then the device went silent. We tried to make it work again but it did not respond.

Time must have passed unusually quickly without us noticing for just then Jill came back with bags of groceries.

"God, I think everyone has decided to go shopping today. I managed to get three fresh rabbit pies. Watch out for the lead shot though. They'll take your fillings out...oh!"

She had noticed our unease. "Sorry, have I interrupted something? You look like you've just been caught doing something you shouldn't."

Before I could answer she noticed me with the telephone. "Ah! You've found Jim's harmigraph? He's been promising to connect that up for over a year. Weird thing is though; I'd swear blind that I've heard strange crackling sounds coming from it. Almost like voices."

Instead of changing the subject as perhaps I would have done, James pursued it and said, "When was this?"

"Well, actually when I come to think about it, usually when you're away. Why?"

"Did you try talking to it?"

"Jim! There's only room for one idiot in this house. It's not connected to anything, remember? And why for heaven's sake are you looking at me like that?"

James looked at me and raised his eyebrows and said, "Because just before you came in someone was talking to us on it."

Jill dropped her bags and sat down.

"OK, Jim. I give up. What's happening now? Is it another thing to do with time? Who was it?"

"It was H. G. Wells"

"What, the science fantasy writer? So he just happened to call you from a hundred years ago on a wireless thingamajig just when you arrive back? Is he off the rails, Elizabeth, or is it me?"

I sympathised with her incredulity. I could see on this occasion that it was quite easy to draw such a conclusion.

I took her hand and said, "No, well no more than normal. What James said was true."

"OK, get the bottle and tell me from the beginning."

We all sat down with large glasses of what Jill called wine but which in truth I can only describe as an alcoholic brew of elderberries or raspberries. James began.

"It's a long story. But basically Wells seems to keep turning up in our hour of need."

I interjected, "I'm not convinced he completely satisfies our needs. In fact his solution seems to further complicate our plight every time he appears."

"OK. I've got that. So what did he say to you both this time?"

"He told us to look for Marco."

"Marco! The one who persuaded me to sit in that blooming submarine contraption? You're on your own on this one, Jim."

Just then the telephone, or as Jill called it, the harmigraph began to crackle. James leapt to it and shouted into the device. "If that's you again, Wells you can b--ger off!"

Before I could admonish James on his choice of language another familiar voice came from the grille. "Thank God! It's you, Urquhart. It's Marco. You've got to help me!"

--- ~ ---

J.

All I wanted to do was have a nice rest and live quietly with Elizabeth in our cottage. Instead here was the other cause of all our trouble back again begging for help. I would have put the phone down except good old Wells had indicated to us that if we wanted to get out of this time line we needed Marco. The trouble was Wells in his usual inscrutable fashion hadn't mentioned how Marco was going to help us. There was one thing though. Wells seemed to be taking an unusual interest in us which suggested he had an agenda. I turned to the telephone.

"Where are you, Marco?"

"I'm at Midhurst."

"And how did you get here? I thought we sent you to the future."

"I found a device in the box containing your diaries"

"You found our diaries! Have you got them with you?"

"No, I put them back."

"Thanks a lot, Marco."

"I didn't need them. The device had it all recorded"

I wondered whether he had the device Wells had given us. But first I needed to know what Marco was up to.

"So back to my question. How did you get back here?"

"I was just thinking about Midhurst while reading the diaries and it happened. The device somehow transported me."

I heard a sharp intake of breath from Elizabeth. I put my finger to my lips for silence. It definitely sounded like the one Wells had, or a copy.

"So what you going to do with it now?"

"Nothing! It sent me here but didn't come with me."

He then told me his story of his demise at the Weber Institute and how he had found it in Rollinson's office with our diaries. He had escaped by just thinking about where we were and hey presto, he found himself back in Midhurst.

Was this another fabrication? You couldn't tell with Marco. I was sure given half the chance he would try and grab his time machine and restart the servers.

"OK, so let's pretend we go along with your story. How did you know where we are?"

"Easy I went to the local Telegraph Office, gave them your name and address and after an extraordinary amount of time while they pulled and pushed plugs around a big electronic board I made contact."

"Good story, Marco. The only slight problem is that this phone is not connected to anything."

There was now silence and just as I thought he'd vanished like Wells, his voice sounding almost scared.

"I don't understand. Then how can I be talking to you?"

I had some understanding but I wasn't going to share it with Marco. This was the phone I had bought from Wells. I wouldn't be surprised if the devious imp, to use Elizabeth's description, was listening. I decided to keep the conversation short.

"I don't know, Marco, but I suggest we meet up. Tomorrow lunch time at the Coaching Inn?"

"Yes, er, Yes, OK. See you there."

The phone rang off. Before I put it down I shouted into the mouthpiece. "Are you there, Wells?'

There was no answer.

--- ~ ---

E.

First a new future, then Mr Wells and now Mr Batalia arrives. We did not seem to have control of anything. It was as though we were being manipulated by some unseen being. I had discussed this before with James. It was my belief that we had no free will. It was if..... I turned to James and Jill and tried to explain this again. My voice was quiet and shaking a little.

"What I'm going to say I hope is not true. But I am beginning to feel more and more unreal. Do you both not feel this?"

They were silent but attentive. I tried to continue.

"It is as if we are just characters in a play. No, it is a book. A book that is not finished!"

"But you could say that about life," said James.

"Yes, but there are our diaries. We have assumed that they record our actions. But is it the reverse? Are we carrying out the actions in the diaries?"

Jill put her hand on my knee. "But if that were true then we are just puppets and if we are just puppets who is the puppet master?"

"God, it could be the Martians!" said James grabbing the line of the argument. "They certainly know how to get into our minds."

22

"Or..." I said, "It could be Mr Wells. He writes books of fantasy and has a great interest in time travel. He could be experimenting with us for a new novel."

Jill stood up. "OK I'm definitely going mad pursuing this. You are now suggesting everything we are saying or doing is the product of someone else's mind."

"I cannot believe it is true either but if it were, then to follow this to a logical conclusion, the puppet master, as you say, may be making it up as he, she, or it goes along."

"God, then it wouldn't know where or when this is going to end!" said James. "Even worse maybe it doesn't know we exist!"

"Maybe our actions are feeding into its mind and it is writing it down in our diaries thinking that our actions are its own ideas!"

My brain was close to fever but then Jill thankfully ended this spiral down to an illogical abyss.

"OK, OK, stop! We are now in the realms of complete fantasy with no proof of anything!"

But James did not stop. "Yes, it's mad but let's say, for the sake of argument, that we are just characters in a book, where does that lead us?"

"God knows. But to answer your question we would need first to contact the Puppet Master or author. But who is it?"

At that moment I recalled what Mr Wells had said on the telephone.

"Was Wells suggesting that was what we should do?"

"What, Marco?" said Jill. "You're saying he is the puppet master? If I get hold of him I'll cut his strings."

"I don't think he's the one, Jill." said James "He doesn't strike me as a controller of anything. I think Marco is just a link. Remember he's a fugitive. I've still got my money on Wells."

--- ~ ---

J.

Before we went further I needed to decide whether Jill should know that we weren't quite the ones she had left two days ago. But first this required understanding how different she was to the Jill we'd left.

"Jill, I need a recap for sanity's sake. Do you mind telling us what we were doing before we left you last? In fact could you just recount briefly how and where Elizabeth and I met?"

"Is this some test, Jim?"

"No. It's just nothing is making sense and I just want to hear that I'm not dreaming."

She went through the story. Everything seemed to fit, even the air police and the abolition of religion; except she had no recall of the Martian invasion.

Then I remembered what Wells had said about this world. I asked Jill for the local paper.

She handed it over to me. The headlines were about the reopening of the Chichester Arun canal and a new tram line to run alongside it. But the picture in the paper was no holiday canal. This one reminded me of the Manchester Ship Canal. There were pages of photos of the opening. But what struck me was the absence of cars, there were only trams. Another page had an article on the extension of the Hothampton Pier on Chichester Plage to accommodate larger boats. Apart from these though the rest were the usual articles on charities, sport and festivals. Then I looked at the advertising section. There were no cars for sale. It looked like Herr Benz and Mr Ford had not captured the public's imagination here.

Now here we were with all three of us thinking we knew each other but actually from different pasts and futures. Each time we moved in time we came back on a slightly different future. The people we returned to had changed a little. But what was beginning to worry me, and I could see it was bothering Elizabeth as well, was: did we change also? Were we the same people with the same memories? I needed to find out. But before I could discuss this with Jill I needed to talk to Elizabeth on her own.

But first some dinner. Thanks to the wine it was about nine o'clock before we ate. There's not a lot you can do with rabbit. No matter which way you cook it, it tastes like rabbit.

After I made excuses that we were very tired and it was time for bed.

--- ～ ---

E.

To be in our bed again. The warmth and comfort with James.

But as I begun to snuggle up he looked at me rather strangely and said,

"Do you remember when we first met?"

I looked at his face. There was almost fear written there.

"Why yes. At Hamgreen. You showed me your watch and then you took photographs of us."

He visibly relaxed.

"Why do you ask?"

I wanted to know you were still my first Elizabeth."

Before I could answer he said, "Elizabeth. We need to pretend that nothing has changed for Jill. It is the only world she knows, and I don't think we should try suggesting that

25

there are hundreds of other Jill's travelling along different time paths."

I thought this was best and agreed. I loved Jill and I didn't want her to think that the Jill we had known lived in a different world. She would not trust us. But I must admit that in agreeing I felt a little deceitful.

James said, "Then to make it easier for us I think we have to learn to live in this world. From the little I've seen it seems to be a little utopia without war or famine. You know, like William Morris's 'News from Nowhere."

"I do not know this, James." I was now very much snuggled up against him. His aroma wafted over me.

"Ah. He realised what you were trying to achieve in the 1870s. A novel about an idyllic world."

"Like the Pre-Raphaelites?"

"Yes, he wanted to create their dream. Remember my wallpaper?"

"Oh yes. It was idyllic."

Idyllic. The word suffused through my mind. I caressed his neck. I felt him begin to relax.

"So we pretend we have always lived in her world?"

"Yes, James."

I pulled him a little closer. At last he melted into my arms.

--- ～ ---

Chapter Two

J.

We rose for breakfast about eight and quickly realised we didn't know where anything was in the kitchen. As I rummaged through drawers and cupboards Jill appeared at the kitchen door.

"Hello, Elizabeth. Have a good sleep? By the way, I like your skirt especially all that green embroidery. Which is more than I can say for you, Jim. You look like a spiv who's had a bad night on the pot and lost his shirt."

I desisted from replying in the manner appropriate for a sibling.

Then she noticed what I was doing. "Are you alright, Jim? You look like you've lost something."

"Sorry. Still not half awake from our travels. I was wondering what to have for breakfast. How long have we been away?"

"Two days, remember? I got you some porridge and fresh milk."

I looked around the kitchen hoping I could guess where she'd put them.

"God, Jim! Sit down. I'll make some for you. You'll have to stop spoiling him, Elizabeth. If you're not careful, you'll be waiting on him hand and foot."

I grinned the grin of a helpless man who can't do anything without a woman's help and sat down.

After breakfast I reminded them we needed to get to Marco at Midhurst. Unfortunately with no cars I needed to know how, and that would mean asking Jill, who would wonder why I didn't know.

I dived in. "What's the best way to get to Midhurst, Jill?"

She looked at me. "Well, you could walk or you could borrow a couple of donkeys from Ron Brewer's field out the back."

"OK, good one but since we've been away for all I know Chichester might have sunk into the sea."

"No, Jim, the trams are still running."

With that information safely extracted I moved on to money.

"Could you lend us some money, Jill? We've only got Victorian cash with us.''

"What do you want money for? Do you want to get arrested? Your ration cards are still in that drawer. With your frugal lifestyle you should have accumulated a fair amount. Some new clothes would be a start."

I went over to the drawer and pulled out a wad of multi-coloured coupon cards for food, clothing and TramsPort. There were also two identity cards. The photo on mine looked like me. I wondered what my job was. I turned it over slowly and read 'Planetarium Supervisor'. A stroke of luck. I could bluff that one though I wondered how much they knew about stars. Then I turned to Elizabeth's. Oh dear, it seems she was a housekeeper and cleaner. That was going to take a bit of explaining, especially with her accent.

--- ∼ ---

E.

A delight I have discovered with crossing futures is that one acquires a new wardrobe on each arrival. I was glad to see that the fashion of this time allowed the wearing of reasonably comfortable garments which did not require the use of a shoehorn or windlass. I must confess though that I have become accustomed to a 'bra'. At first I was a little reticent by its constrictions but when Jill drew my attention to the shape of the bust acquired by ladies of a certain age who had not worn them during their lives I quickly realised its long-term advantage. However, a good one that is comfortable but does not attract immediate attention is hard to find and in our travels whenever I have found one that 'fits' it has, how can I put this, found its way quickly into my portmanteau.

With regard to my 'new' occupation although my clothing was no longer of the class I was used to I was gratified to find that class by clothing was not apparent on the streets. James, however, did enjoy for a while, taking advantage of my 'new' position by drawing attention at every opportunity to any clutter and dust in our cottage. This game stopped though when I 'cleaned' out his drawer of slide rules and ready reckoners and hid them in the attic. I then let him wander about for an hour looking for them until when he questioned me I said I 'remembered' that I may have been overzealous in my cleaning activities and put them in a safe place for which for the life of me I could not recall. Eventually he guessed my game and said,

"Should I presume, Elizabeth, if I go easy on the reminders to charlady duties it might help you remember where you put them?"

"Mmh." Putting a finger to my forehead and looking towards the ceiling I replied. "You know James I do think such a plan could be quite advantageous in assisting my memory."

But to Midhurst. Jill had left for work. I understood that she was working at the local council offices and her time was fully occupied reviewing plans for the new canal's hydraulics which were to be installed to ensure that the waterway was navigable as far as Arundel and beyond.

We packed some suitable spare clothing in two 'rucksacks' which James provided. Although I would say they were not normally fashionable for the more genteel clientele of Chichester they were practicable and allowed freedom of movement that a travel bag did not have. We also decided to take monies from our own time as our experience had taught us that time often had an unexpected fluidity.

We walked into Chichester along the new canal, already full of commercial barges waiting to unload their wares, to the train station where we boarded an electric tram for Midhurst. Inside it was crowded with what I took to be farm workers and the air was permeated with a smell of leather which reminded me of German towns. A bell rang and the tram started almost unnoticeably then glided silently on rails up North Street which was already full of morning shoppers heading for the Market. This was much more satisfying than James' 'car' and bliss compared with that unspeakable flying contraption we took to the North. After Singleton, where I remembered in another world on certain days hordes of "Cockneys" would arrive from London for the Races, we entered a tunnel. Then out to Cocking and Midhurst. James was thoroughly enjoying this and marvelled how a world could so easily be put to rights if the right heads were banged together.

We had just alighted from the tram and were walking to the old coaching inn when I was sure, out of the corner of my eye, I saw a car cross a road! But unlike the cars of James world it seemed to hover. Then it turned and vanished down a street. I grabbed James' arm.

"James, did you see that?"

"What?"

"A car! It was floating just there. Then it turned down that street."

"Are you sure? Quick!"

We ran to the street but there was nothing there.

"Well, if you really did see it, it's not part of this world. Let's go and find Marco and see what he knows."

--- ~ ---

J.

When we got to the inn we managed to reserve the White Room again, then wandered up and down Church Street waiting for Marco. The shops mainly sold fresh local farm produce, clothes and what my dad used to call ironmongery. No electronic gadget shops unfortunately. I was also struck by the smoothness of the pavements. Not a crack or a broken stone to be seen. No doubt due to the absence of any cars or delivery vans. In my time most pavements were falling apart due to the common practice of 'people in a hurry' straddling the pavements with their vehicles rather than finding a proper car park.

The lack of any sign of transport vehicles was beginning to worry me a little. How did all the goods get to the shops? In another age without vehicles the road would have been full of carts and workers but not here. Yet there were plenty of goods on display. As we could use some new clothes I thought I could find out how the system worked.

We went into a men's clothes shop which also served as a barber, judging by the striped pole fixed to the wall outside. There was a smell of leather and wool. The clothes were, how can I put this, functional and workman like. You could have anything you wanted, provided it was a black or grey woollen suit. The proprietor, who was wearing a striped shirt with braces, was busy adding up a list of handwritten numbers. When he saw me he stopped writing, folded the paper and inserted it into a cylindrical flask which he pushed into a glass vacuum tube. He then pulled a wire. A bell rang and the cylinder with a hiss shot up the tube and vanished through the wall where I presumed there was a back office.

He looked up. "Can I help, sir? You have the appearance of a man who needs some new clothes."

Sensing a losing argument coming I decided to agree.

We went round the shop picking up items which I needed. Or should I say items which Elizabeth thought I should need. When I felt the moment was right I asked,

"So who makes your clothes?"

"Manchester. Delivered every Friday night. Brought down by barge. How else?"

"Oh, sorry, I thought they might be made locally."

"Tried it. Not wet enough. North has all the rain and damp. Easier for spinning."

"So how do you get them to your shop?"

He looked at me rather strangely.

"Look, I just work here. Everything's here when I come in on Saturday morning"

"But how do they get from the barges?"

"Not for me to know. My job is selling. That's all."

Then he showed me his identity card. It said 'Shop Keeper'. He was looking at me rather suspiciously now as though I was some kind of inspector checking up on him.

"Sorry. Just curious. Been away for a long time."

"Are you buying anything?"

I bought a couple of shirts, trousers and underwear and a jacket. I gave him my clothes coupons and he removed about a third of it.

As I was about to leave wearing a new woollen charcoal suit, Elizabeth suggested that although I thought Victorians only changed their underwear once a year and sowed themselves in for the winter it would be rather nice if she could make an exception and replenish some of her clothes.

--- ~ ---

E.

James was quite surprised to find that the ladies' department was upstairs above the gentlemen's clothing store. I reminded him that in my era ladies clothing was kept on the first floor so gentlemen would not inadvertently come across them. I still remember the shock of walking into the ground floor of an emporium in Chichester where all manner of ladies' garments and unmentionables were on display for ALL to see! Not to mention mannequins in the shop windows so scantily dressed that I am sure even the most resolute gentleman would have difficulty giving his wife or fiancée due attention in front of such objects.

James agreed and said that if that lingerie department where we had found him examining personal 'items' in Chichester had been on the first floor an embarrassing encounter may have been avoided.

I do think sometimes he doesn't even try to defend his misdemeanours. But then I must remember he was brought up in a society that was much more laissé faire in this area than mine. I am sure if I asked him to buy undergarments for me it would be a trifle to him.

Anyway, to return to the shop and the ladies' department. After the pleasure of lycra and chemically created garments it was almost disappointing to find clothing of natural material again. I discovered there was no cotton only wool, flax and leather, which are not the most comfortable against the flesh. When I enquired about silk, the proprietor regarded James and his coupons and suggested that if he was frugal with his spending habits and he came back in a couple of years he might find a 'little something' which we could afford. Despite James' generous offer of a down payment which was rather brusquely refused, I decided that in future I would make an effort to 'squirrel away' any clothing which did not feel that one was doing penance in a Trappist monastery.

After leaving the shop we promenaded along Church Street and looked in at Wells' old Chemist Shop in the hope of meeting him but to no avail and so we continued to the Inn. At this point James brought up the topic of the shop keeper and the delivery of his wares in an oblique way.

"Did you notice anything strange about the barges on the canal?"

I said I had not noticed anything unusual, but I was too preoccupied in trying to understand the time in which we were travelling.

"Yes, me too. But thinking back. They were all parked but no one was taking anything off."

This did not seem unusual.

"Maybe they carry out the work at night so as to ensure stocks are full for the following day. Certainly in my day, many tradesmen were up by two or three in the morning to ensure their wares were ready for the City going to work. I know some of the clerks employed by my uncle's firm in the city must walk three or four miles each day and are up at four and not returned until eight in the evening."

"Yeah, you could be right, Elizabeth. But I'd like to see how it's done. And that car you said you saw worries me."

Just then Mr Batalia appeared at the same time as we arrived at the Inn. He looked harassed. He seemed to have abandoned his creaseless suit and acquired clothing of a form often seen worn by James on a Sunday morning after an exceedingly late evening with the port.

--- ~ ---

J.

Last time I saw Marco he was getting into the time machine at Midhurst in the hope of getting back to ComsMesh.

"So why do you want to see us, Marco?"

"I told you. I just thought about you and here I am."

"The only problem is with so many different futures, how do you know if we are the Urquharts and Bicesters you are looking for?"

There was a look of shock on his face. I carried on.

"In fact, Marco, how do you know you've actually left? Maybe your real self is now locked up somewhere and you are just some copy. One of many hundreds or thousands of copies."

"That's ridiculous. If that were true we would never know who we really are!"

"Precisely. Do you know Wells told us that he personally didn't travel in time? He visited the future as out of body experiences. Maybe all we've been through is just such a dream?"

Elisabeth was appalled by this. "Good God, James! If that were true we have only met through a dream state and we are really just home asleep! I have never really been with you!"

I gently pulled her to me and half whispered in her ear.

"Well, if that's the case you're the best dream I've ever had and I hope it never ends."

--- ～ ---

E.

This path we were now taking was laced with laudanum. Whether we were real or not we could not escape. We had to play out our parts and make what sanity we could out of this madness. But like James if it was a dream I did not want the dream to end.

Wells is the key. He told us to meet Mr Batalia and then inexplicably shortly afterwards Mr Batalia contacted us. And now we are together and in Midhurst. I can only think that any clues to an exit from this maze must be with the time cavern beneath the old castle. Though how that will help I do not know for we had shut down the time machine power source on our previous visit. But first I needed to understand Mr Batalia intentions. I had to be careful in my enquiries for I did not trust him, and never will.

"Mr Batalia, or whoever you are, pray tell why you wished to contact us? If I recall correctly you made great haste to leave us at our last meeting. Are you looking for your time machine?"

I could tell this hit the mark and I was pleased to see an admiring glance from James.

"OK, I admit I'm looking for the machine."

James said, "Why do you want the machine, Marco?"

"Because I believe it is lodged in our original time line. And if we can find it we can all get back to our time."

I was not convinced by this argument. Mr Batalia had said he that when he had returned in the time machine from Midhurst his world had changed. But I felt in order to progress we had to play his game. A little portrayal of feminine weakness perhaps would help.

"In that case, we will go to the cavern again for I am quite desperate to be back in my own time again. Are you not also, James?"

As I said this I moved over to James and placed my arm around him in the pretence of a hug and signalled to him by a slight pinch to his waist. Unfortunately he misread my intention and responded with a similar movement but then slowly slid his hand inside the rear of my skirt until I felt his hand on my flesh!

I confess I found it rather difficult to continue to regard Mr. Batalia with due interest. In fact it took all my nerve not to withdraw his hand instantly and turn around to see if any passer-by had noticed!

I later pointed out to James that it was not good manners to grope one's wife in public. Nor, in reply to his immediate response, was it acceptable to grope any other person's wife. Really! However, when pressed he rather weakly claimed his hand had slid into my skirts by mistake but once there, noticing I made no protest he thought he would stay there. Questioned on this poor argument he tried to make amends by saying that I shouldn't have such a nice bottom!

Only James could get away with it. But I digress again. It was agreed to visit the cavern immediately and go by way of the crypt in the church. Midhurst Castle looked exactly as it had done on our original time line, low ruined walls partly hidden by the shrubbery next to the church. When we arrived at the church door we found it locked, but by chance the vestry door opened with a 'little' assistance from James' shoulder.

The nave looked as though it had not been visited in years. Dusty pews and furniture were piled in broken heaps against the wall and bibles and prayer books were scattered on the floors. The place was obviously no longer a place of worship. This impression was reinforced by the sound of pigeons flying about in the roof overhead and their guano on the ledges of the broken windows. We carefully walked across the broken floor and descended the short flight of stone steps to the crypt. The door to the cavern tunnel was still there but across it lay the remains of the psaltery which required some effort from all three of us to move. The door, luckily, was held by a simple latch. Remembering some of our previous escapades I asked if either of them had a torch and received an expected answer coupled with embarrassment. However, Mr Batalia produced a small gas 'lighter' which he thought would be of use.

James immediately picked up some prayer books and proceeded to rip out wads of sheets to form a torch. Although I was not particularly religious I had regularly attended church and found this quite shocking. It was difficult not to regard this as a sacrilegious act which would revisit us at a later time. Nevertheless I said nothing. However, when he picked up a bible I had to intervene. James understood immediately and put it down with a small sigh.

Mr Batalia noticed this and rather sardonically questioned my beliefs.

"Still expecting God is waiting for you in one of these time futures, Mrs Urquhart?"

I gave him no quarter.

"Sir, please do not make light of my beliefs. I may have difficulty with my faith but one thing I try to avoid is tempting fate and tearing up the bible .....well, it is too good a book to be treated as such. Now shall we return to this door?"

--- ~ ---

J.

The door opened easily and by the faint light from the nave I could see the tunnel. Marco and I eventually made two torches from the prayer books, but the paper was damp and they only held their light for a moment. It was at this point Elizabeth appeared, I prepared myself for an appropriate comment from her on our pyrotechnic abilities. She contented herself with silently handing over four candles!

"Will these be any good James? I thought, unlike the prayer books, they are more suitably fashioned for the purpose of giving light."

She had that demure expression on her face of the innocent young girl which she used sometimes when I hadn't quite come up to expectations. I should have known she'd get me back for that grope.

"And where did you get those?" I said, trying not to notice the smouldering embers of my 'torch' which had now reached my fingers' tips.

She then pointed at a small altar table at the end of the crypt which looked like it had enough candles to light all the saints for the rest of the year.

We stuffed some extra candles in our pockets and entered the tunnel. The earthen floor was unmarked indicating no one had been there for a long time. The walls were bare save for the pick marks of the tunnel maker. I wouldn't be surprised if it was as old as the Castle.

After about fifty yards the tunnel bent to the right and there was the door. It was smooth, grey or bronze in the candlelight with no obvious handle. I pushed as gently as I could and nearly jumped out my skin as I watched my hand go straight through the door!

After I had calmed down Marco said. "It must be a force field or something like it, absorbing light. All we have to do is walk through it."

"Are you serious? How do you know it's not just one way? It's not of my world. Is it from yours?"

"No. Never seen anything like it. But I haven't come all this way just to turn back now."

And with that he walked through the door and vanished!

I shouted. "Marco, Marco! Are you there?"

No answer. I turned to Elizabeth.

"Well, James, are we turning back or are we going to find what we are looking for?"

I don't know where she gets her courage from. It certainly wasn't from me. I held her hand tightly and stepped into the door.

--- ~ ---

Addendum

Weber Institute, Mons Olympus, Mars
Report 2023a.12.6.15
Earthside breach: Field Portal 3337

Two breaches of the space-time boundary have occurred. Presumed caused by sentient creatures. Sensors indicate creatures are using combustible material for illumination suggesting entry was via Fossil Time Line 23.

Creatures on this time line are not regarded as threat priority.

Report 2023a.12.6.18

Unusual time distortion sensed in proximity of Portal 23. space-time boundary at entry returned to normal suggesting time aberration caused by creatures. Conclude the presence of time-space controller. If confirmed then creatures not from TimeLine 23 but Wellsian TimeLine 21. Analysis required from ComsMesh.

Report 2023a.12.6.18d

ComsMesh conclude time distortion is from transponder removed by Batalia at Weber Institute Earthside. However, additional distortions detected in two of the creatures. These are Wellsian in character and suggest these creatures are out of time and therefore may not be controllable.

--- ~ ---

Chapter Three

E.

We stood in an orange desert under a hazy sky speckled with stars. A small moon was rising and a dazzling yellow star shone, casting shadows on the landscape. In the distance, mountains or cliffs rose impossibly high above a thin white mist which rose where the star light shone. It was beautiful.

Then I noticed we were inside what looked like an observatory with a glass canopy but there was no evidence of the time machine that had previously occupied the room. I turned to James but as I moved towards him I felt strangely light as though a weight had lifted from me. It was impossible but I knew where we were.

"Is this Mars, James?"

"Yes, I think so and for some reason we've landed in a room built for humans. Because if it is Mars, then out there," he pointed to the desert, "Our blood would boil within minutes."

I tried to imagine this and failed. It was then that I realised that Marco was missing.

"But where is Marco?"

We both quickly looked around the room. There was no one, just four doors, one of which had provided our entrance.

"He must have vanished through one of those doors. Damn! Can you remember which one we came through, Elizabeth?"

I hesitated then pointed to one. James walked slowly to it and pushed first his hand with the candle and then, rather bravely I thought, his head through the door.

"Yes. that's our tunnel. I could see our footsteps in the dust. Well spotted. I'll leave a candle next to this door as a marker."

I then suggested that we should try each door in turn to see where they led but James was reluctant.

"Elizabeth, I'm not ready for this yet. I'm sorry but I need to get back into our world for a while to think this through and there's another thing."

This was not like James. Normally I could rely on his foolhardiness to overcome his lack of courage.

"What, James? We have come too far to turn back now."

"Marco has the lighter. If these candles go out we'll be in pitch black."

I could not argue with this. I thought of those Martian creatures at Helmsley silently creeping up unseen on us in the dark and shuddered. And so, I agreed, and we passed through the door and into our tunnel.

As we reached the crypt James said. "We need to plan this properly. But first we need to gather up as many candles as we can and take them back to the door. I'd like a backup supply along our route."

We placed bundles of candles next to the door and James pushed about a dozen through it into the Martian observatory. Then we returned to the inn and our room.

The small door through which we had entered on our previous adventures, I was glad to see, was still there.

James said, "Let's first get something to eat. We might as well fortify ourselves before we indulge in more madness. I wonder what I can get with these food coupons."

I suddenly felt hungry.

$--- \sim ---$

J.

The meal was plain and well-seasoned with salt. It was straight out of my grandmother's cookbook. Few greens but plenty of swede, carrots and parsnips. It wasn't until I finished that I noticed there were no potatoes. I wondered whether America had been discovered. The beef, however, was delicious and tasted like real cow.

Unfortunately the beer was rather weak. Possibly no more than two percent and tasting of hops. However, it went down well. Elizabeth noticed and rather helpfully suggested that I should order another to test its consistency. A perfect wife!

I paid with the coupons and then looked for a shop that would sell matches. I found one which reminded me of my uncle's ironmongers he had had when I was a child. It was an Aladdin's Cave of junk. Pots, pans, buckets and wooden utensils lined dusty shelves. It smelt of paraffin and meths. I decided to take the opportunity to stack up. I bought four boxes of matches, a flint, a penknife, a 30-yard ball of thick string and anything else I could remember a small boy scout might need.

Elizabeth was rather intrigued.

"I can see now, James, how Henry's house accumulated its curios. So this is what boys are like when left to their own devices without the constraints of a female."

I replied, rather foolishly in hindsight, "And I have seen what girls' bedrooms are like without the constraints of a man to temper their desires."

"Really, James? And how many ladies' boudoirs have you visited? And more to the point what desires have you tempered?"

There was a twinkle in her eye. She turned my words round so well.

"Oh, hundreds, Elizabeth. I only married you because I couldn't face visiting another one."

"Well, I am glad I have saved all those women from further compromise and they can now sleep safely in their beds. But enough of your secret fantasies. We had better return to our adventure before you are tempted by your desires."

We went back to the church armed with two bags of my 'essential' survival kit and went down the tunnel to the door. I picked up some more candles from the crypt. You can never have enough candles.

The observatory, as Elizabeth called it, looked exactly the same. However, the small moon had disappeared and what I took to be our sun was higher in the sky. The mist against the hill had evaporated. I was relieved to find the candles were where I had left them.

We now had to deal with the other three doors. I placed one candle by the first, two by the second and three by the third.

Elizabeth then gently reminded me I now had two doors with one candle. I quickly added a candle to each of the three new doors.

"Well, which first, Elizabeth?"

She answered by going to the first door on the opposite wall and slowly pushed her lighted candle and then her head through the door. I had sudden vision of the door freezing and trapping her, which I quickly suppressed.

Thankfully she withdrew intact.

"James, you must see this!"

I looked through the door and saw an immense cavern. A feeling of vertigo washed over me. We were high up and before us as far as the eye could see were what I could only think of as great spaceships bathed in that green glow we had seen at Helmsley. It was the mind vision I had seen when I connected to the Martian in the castle. But as I looked closer it looked deserted. In fact it looked abandoned. Not a soul was to be seen nor any movement.

"That must be their invasion force, but it looks almost like a museum."

I withdrew back into the observatory and tried the third door. I pulled back immediately.

It was the same cavern! But in this one there was a hive of activity. Martians were everywhere!

We turned to the fourth one. The same cavern with all the dockyard machinery but the ships had gone! This was madness.

"I feel, James, I have just looked at three different tableaux of a place. It is almost as though we are looking at different times in its construction. Do you think that is what we are seeing?"

We looked through the three doors again and were greeted by the same views.

"It could be three different points in time, but it could also be three different futures."

"So, if I understand correctly, these doors could allow us to enter three different time lines. There could be hundreds of these doors, James. Perhaps we could find the one that takes us home?"

Her deductive powers amaze me, and I'm supposed to be the logical scientist. However, where do we start? I looked around the observatory again. There were only four doors.

"We are here with a choice. Retreat back down the tunnel or enter one of these doors. Any preference, Elizabeth?"

$--- \sim ---$

E.

My preference was to run back to the warmth of the inn. I think that was James' as well but we both knew this would resolve nothing.

I said, "Let us presume by the absence of footprints that Mr Batalia didn't go back down the tunnel and has gone through one of these doors. Now, if we also presume that he saw the same visions as us then his choice would be influenced by his motives."

"Which was to find the time machine and get back to his own world."

"Yes. But I do not know why. Perhaps he wanted to stop the invasion."

"Then he would choose a door which was before the invasion in the hope of preventing it? That is ambitious, Elizabeth. He doesn't strike me as one for playing heroics. Quite the opposite, in fact."

"I agree, James. Mr Batalia did not strike me as an adventurer or an honourable man. In fact, he was prone to run away at the least difficulty."

"I have quite some sympathy with that. The only difference is I never seem to get the opportunity to leg it."

He looked a little dejected. Encouragement was needed. James was not a hero, nor did I look for that in him, I hasten to say. Usually such people had short lives and those that didn't, spent their lives embellishing their heroic deeds to the detriment of the gullible who tried to follow in their footsteps.

I decided to try a different tack.

"I think I understand two of the futures. Would you say the hive of activity is the Martians preparing for invasion, and the second where there are no flying machines is when they have already left to invade Earth?"

"Yes; that would make sense but what about the third where the cavern is deserted with the ships still there?"

"Perhaps they are waiting for the invasion or perhaps the invasion has been abandoned?"

"And that's the one Marco thinks is his world! Because in his original world the Martians hadn't invaded. God, you're a genius!"

I then received quite an unexpected embrace which I was pleased to say did not include a wandering hand into my garments again and an impressionable and rather forceful kiss full on my lips and the shock almost prevented me returning it with equal vigour. Eventually I had to push James gently away because I began to feel, dare I say, that if he asked to return to the inn rather than go through the door at that moment I would have found it difficult not to acquiesce.

"Gosh, James! You have left me quite flustered. I must be more careful with my bright ideas in future. So shall we go?"

--- ~ ---

J.

Despite the green glow illuminating the cavern we decided to take as many candles as we could carry. I also thought I'd follow Ariadne's idea and use them as markers if we found ourselves in any labyrinths. The first problem, however, was how to get down to the floor of the cavern. From what I could remember the gravity on Mars was a little under fifty percent of Earth's. So I reckon for a given drop we would fall at half the speed and therefore we could fall at least twice as far with the same effect when we hit ground. We would also be about half the weight which meant we wouldn't need the same muscle power to hold on to things to break our descent. I explained this to Elizabeth.

"So, James, I believe we are about fifty feet above the ground which at home would ensure a quick death whereas here it is likely to ensure just crippling injuries. I am not quite sure which I prefer."

"Well, this is where my ball of string might come in useful if it is strong enough."

"You are not seriously going to lower us down on that?"

"Yes."

I could see this was going to take a little persuading.

I untwined it and giving her one end we gave it a good yank to test its strength. It held! I don't know what it was made of. It looked and smelt like hemp.

"OK, Elizabeth. I'm going to tie this round your waist and lower you down. It should be easy. You'll only weigh about four stone."

I hoped I'd guessed her weight right. Girls can get quite uppity on this subject.

The tying round her waist was more difficult than I expected, not helped by her reluctance to join in.

"Are you sure I haven't done something unforgivable to you, James, because please tell me and I will apologise profusely."

"It'll be alright, Elizabeth. Trust me. It'll be just like climbing down a tree. Look. There are various conduits criss-crossing the wall which will give something to grab hold of and I'll be keeping the string tight."

She looked at me one more time then holding my hand clambered over the edge. I then slowly played out the string and she descended down the wall. I was quite impressed with her agility and hoped I would be just as good. When she got to the bottom I got her to untie it. Then I retrieved it and used it to lower our baggage. Then it was my turn. The flaw in my plan then revealed itself. I could not find anything to tie the string to.

At this point Elizabeth became rather animated. She was trying to say something and pointing but I couldn't hear or see what she was on about. No doubt she was referring to my stupidity in checking for a hold point.

There was only one thing left to do. Drop down and try and grab the pipework to break my speed. The first pipe was about ten feet away. I lowered myself over the edge until I was dangling by my hands. Just four feet to go. I let go. I slowly fell and my feet landed on the pipe perfectly and then slipped off! As I passed the pipe I grabbed it and luckily managed to hang on. Unluckily, the pipe didn't support my weight and snapped. I was then treated to a slow swing towards the ground as I held on to the end of the pipe and landed with an undignified bump which could have been worse. When I looked up I saw Elizabeth standing over me who surprisingly offered no sympathy.

"You idiot, James, could you not hear me? You gave me such a fright with your foolhardiness. Look!"

And she pointed to the wall where what looked like a ladder or climbing frame went up to the side of the door.

--- ～ ---

E.

It was brave of James to try and guess my weight. It is generally accepted that once a lady achieves a certain maturity, which apparently can occur before she realises it has arrived, that it is unwise to guess and inform her of her weight or age as this normally results in disappointment if not argument.

I later mentioned this to James who agreed this was a 'dangerous' field to explore but he had presumed by the absence of comment he may have been 'lucky' with his estimation on this occasion. He said that he had also learnt not to assume a woman of a certain size was with child as he had first-hand experience of a friend who made this assumption. Apparently in an effort to demonstrate his manners, his friend had offered such a lady a seat on a train and then by way of polite conversation enquired as to her health and that of the child to be. The altercation that followed necessitated both he and his friend alighting from the train at the next available station to await the next.

However, this was a trifle compared to his suggestion to throw me off the wall! I agreed only because he managed to convince me that he knew what he was doing. Why I came to that conclusion I am still not quite sure as 'knowing what he is doing' is not always his strong point. I do sometimes worry that although it is, according to Jill, generally agreed that the female of our race is accepted as superior to what is called the 'other half', we do at times seem too susceptible to their 'persuasive' powers for our own good. But I keep that to myself for he always tries to do his best and with few exceptions they are for my benefit. This, however, was not completely apparent on this occasion.

Luckily the string held. It was only as I descended that I noticed the ladder. Unfortunately I was too preoccupied with the fear of falling to point this out until I was safe on Terra Firma or in this case Mars Firma.

$$---\sim---$$

J.

There was no sign of Marco nor thankfully any of the Martians. With no plan we decided to have a look at the nearest spaceship. I remembered to place a candle by the ladder as a marker. As we approached the ship it became more and more apparent that it was derelict. Many of the hatches were half open and machinery and equipment lay scattered around it. I identified what looked like an entrance port. The circular door was wedged half open by a piece of pipe. We climbed up some steps and looked in to what seemed to be a narrow horizontal shaft. We could not see very far and, after listening for any sound, lit candles and entered the shaft. It emerged into an oval room. A control centre perhaps. In the light of the candles our shadows flickered eerily large on the walls which my imagination kept interpreting as Martian. I could see equipment and furniture scattered over the floor and panels had been ripped out of consoles. Just as I approached what looked like the helm I heard Elizabeth catch her breath. I turned instantly round and saw her staring at something by a seat.

"James, I think I have found a Martian."

There by the chair was the remains of a skeleton. It certainly looked about the size of a Martian. The skull almost rabbit-like if a rabbit had three eye sockets. I didn't want to touch in case it had some residual telepathic controls.

We backed away slowly all the time listening for any sound. Our shadows followed us. Then I noticed another shaft or corridor. By the light of the candles we could see it led into a long chamber. We looked at each other and then, placing another candle on the floor entered, holding hands. Inside there were rows of transparent pods. Many were open, their oval lids raised. With some trepidation we walked along the aisle between the rows. Some were empty but every few pods there was a Martian skeleton. Judging by their contortions they had not died peacefully. Near the end, by what seemed to be an exit port, dozens of skeletons lay jumbled as though there had been a panic to get out. I carefully stepped between them and looked through the port. Across the ground I could just make out here and there more skeletons.

"This is a place of untimely death, James. What time or future have we joined?"

"I think I know what this is. This is not an abandoned invasion. This is the remnants of the invasion force after the biological attack on Earth. Those that escaped must have brought the disease back here and what we see is the panic that ensued."

"That means, James, that those three doors lead to the same time line. We are witnessing then, the preparation for invasion and this is the aftermath from their defeat."

"I wonder if there are any left. We may have exterminated the whole race. Unless they managed to seal off this chamber."

"Do you think we could be affected? I mean could the disease be here still?"

"From what I can remember they were killed by the common cold so we should be alright."

I crossed my fingers.

So we were now in the Martian invasion time line. But where did we go from here? Marco was nowhere to be seen and he hadn't come back to the tunnel. So what was he looking for?

--- ~ ---

E.

We left the ship and wandered around the cavern. All six ships were in a similar state. I remarked to James that we seemed to be enclosed in an Earth atmosphere as we could breathe quite normally.

At one end of the cavern I could see the outline of a great door through which I thought the ships could travel to the sky. James speculated that it might actually be a force field similar to the doors through which we had passed and possibly also acted as a barrier between the atmosphere here and the Martian surface. Again we could not think of any reason why the Martians would keep this cavern's atmosphere like Earth's.

Just then I heard the faint sound of a tinkling bell and turned to find James was looking at his phone again.

"Elizabeth, I'm getting a signal! Good God, I've got GPS!"

I had read a little on this navigational system run by satellites that float above the Earth like Platonic souls when I was trying to understand relativity with James. It is a wonder. If I understand correctly, they travel so fast their time or clocks are slowed compared to ours. But because they are subject to less gravity, due to their distance from the Earth, space is bent less and their time is not slowed as much. The result apparently is that their clocks tell a different time to ours and must be corrected if they are to give an accurate navigational position!

I digress on this only because I still do not understand why if their clocks are different to ours we can see them? For surely they are not here in the present? I will save this conundrum for James at a more convenient moment because his discovery of a signal had made him rather animated.

"That's impossible. Unless..."

"What, James?"

"It means we're not on Mars; we're on Earth."

Our whole hypothesis had collapsed.

J.

This was going to require all of our four neurons. I hoped Elizabeth's were talking to each other because mine had gone on holiday.

"So, to recap. When was the last time we thought we were in the world we thought we were in? If you get what I mean."

"I think it was when we stopped those machines at Midhurst because when we returned to your cottage at Chichester we had entered Mr. Wells' world of the Martians."

"Agreed. Then we went to Helmsley as suggested by Wells and found ourselves in 1895."

"And then after that horrific encounter with those creatures, Mr. Wells, using the device, sent us back to what we thought was your time but was a future of gas and no cars."

"Agreed. Then we came to Midhurst, entered the cavern, went through a door to what we thought was Mars and then passed through some other doors and found ourselves with the Martians back on Earth. Simple really. Can't see what the problem is."

"Except the little problem that we do not know where or when we really are."

"Yes. How could I forget?"

"And we have not found Mr. Batalia."

"How silly of me."

"And we also do not know what Mr Wells is doing?"

"Yep. Completely slipped my mind. Speaking of which, do you mind if I go home now?"

"Of course, James. Can I come with you? I've brought my magic shoes."

"Please do. Shall we fly?"

"Why not, James. For I am a little tired now."

"Of course. Let me carry you."

It's surprising how stress gets to you sometimes.

---~---

E.

It took I think over half an hour to clamber through the wreckage to the cavern entrance. We did not talk. Then we stood facing the smooth wall. There was not a mark on it. We looked at each other, then lighting our candles and holding hands we stepped through it.

---~---

End of Part I

Part II

Hot House

Addendum

Weber Institute, Mons Olympus, Mars.

Report 2015c.15.3.9

Earthside: Time-Space World-Line 24.

The destruction of the primary fleet and the servers has awoken Earth to our presence. Their engineers are already examining the wreckage of our ships and tripods. It will not be long before they understand the mode of flight. Their germ pods continue to arrive making much of the surface uninhabitable.

The Martians no longer trust us to save their world. The number of future time lines available is also diminishing and those where ComsMesh have succeeded have closed. The only course available is to increase substantially the level of CO_2 on Earth. Already the ice caps are melting, sea levels are rising and the permafrost is melting releasing vast quantities of methane. It is expected the Atlantic Escalator will soon fail which will bring a new ice age destroying the great industrial northern hemisphere.

$$--- \sim ---$$

Chapter Four

J.

In the summer, on baking hot sky blue afternoons the cliffs of the chalk white Severn Sisters are crowded with holiday makers picnicking and enjoying the view. What's not apparent to most of them is that if they could climb down the face of Seaford Head a little and press themselves against the chalk they would disappear into the wall and enjoy a more fantastic view of the remains of a Martian invasion force.

And so we stood on the beach below the towering white walls feeling the fresh breeze and salt surf spray.

Up above three hang gliders rode the warm rising air.

We walked along the shingled beach letting the tide wet our feet until we reached the mouth of the Cuckmere where we laid on the sand soaking up the sun and each other. After a while I got out my phone and tried to ring Jill.

$$--- \sim ---$$

E.

The relief of hearing Jill's voice again. She came for us by car.

When she got out I must admit for once I found myself relieved to see that she wore a most immodest clinging vest and the shortest skirt which was, no doubt, designed to absorb the maximum sunlight and allow the minimum of imagination.

James being James his first words were.

"What a great car, Jill! Where did you get it?"

"Government initiative. Hydrogen fuel cells."

It was a golden yellow and smooth and bulbous with the window extending around like a dome.

Luckily before James could enter into a discussion on the merits of its lower left-handed manglewurzle sprogget or whatever passed for what Jill called his 'car speak' ... Jill turned her attention to me.

"My God, Elizabeth, who bought you those clothes? Was that your idea, Jim, to make sure you keep her to yourself?"

"You should see her underwear." He quipped with a grin.

"James! Really!"

"You can always rely on Jim to protect a girl's modesty, eh, Elizabeth? By the way, what's that blouse made of? It looks like starched linen or something. As for the colour… I don't think grey really suits you."

She came closer to have a look and then regarding me with a knowing smile whispered.

"Mmmh. You must get Jim to learn how to do your buttons up properly."

I turned to James who just at that moment had taken to studiously looking out to sea.

I liked Jill because she always knew and made no moral judgement.

It was a comfort to have 'normal service' returned.

When we arrived at James' cottage his room had reassuringly returned to its familiar cosiness of books and floral prints and the black screen once again occupied the wall. We sat down and over tea recounted our adventures. For a while Mr Batalia, Mr Wells and their pasts and futures became a foreign country.

---~---

Chapter Five

E.

The next morning our idyllic slumber was woken by Jill asking if we wished to do any Christmas shopping as there were only two weeks to go. The morning temperature did not suggest the season. The window was open, and a warm breeze gently disturbed the curtains. I had presumed it was high summer. I quickly said I would like to join her then got up and looked out into the small garden. Daffodils and crocuses were in full bloom and already the yellow of the forsythia covered the wall! I went back to James and gently woke him with a kiss and put my finger to my lips to indicate that quietness and tact was required. I then drew him to the window.

"I've just discovered it is December, James, and Christmas is near."

I could see he understood immediately. He lowered his head, almost dejected.

"Oh dear. Here we go again. I suppose it's too much to hope that somehow we've been magically transported to Australia. Well, let's go and have breakfast. I guess the same rules for this Jill as well."

--- ~ ---

J.

Chichester was now a small port and Bognor had been transformed into a little Venice.

Despite world governments having managed to virtually eliminate fossil fuel emissions the residual effects of the past had not prevented a rise in temperature and sea levels with

61

massive population shifts as a consequence. The North East coasts had now become a place of choice in the summer where people could cool in the remains of the Arctic breeze.

Global trade had drifted further north with the main routes now crossing the Arctic Seas from the north of Canada to the Arctic coast of Russia.

An unexpected consequence of global warming was the massive green growth in the equatorial world due to increased rainfall and CO_2 which had gone some way to supplement the loss of agriculture in the north.

At breakfast Jill treated us to a full metal English. Bacon, eggs, fried bread and sausages. Perfect. My cholesterol was back in shape. While Elizabeth decided to take a shower I decided to confront Jill full on to try to glean what time line we were on.

"Any more news from the Martians?"

"Not a thing, Jim. The UN is bombing the planet with germ pods but there's been no response. The US and Russia are putting together a fleet using the knowledge they've got from the tripods."

This world was closer to ours.

"What's their plan?"

"Their plan? Their plan is Plan B. A spare new world in their pocket just in case this one goes for a Burton. As you know, the Earth's in bad shape. There's mass migration north. There must be over a billion Indians and Chinese in Siberia now and Antarctica is filling up with Africans and South Americans. A lot of old enemies have become best of mates now that they've realised religion wasn't the key to survival let alone salvation."

"Thank God for science. In another time they'd have been filling the temples praying it would all go away. So our long-term plan is to terraform Mars?"

"Yes. At the moment the atmosphere is too thin and there's too much CO_2, but they can change that with plants."

"But surely plants, although they give off oxygen, absorb most of what they produce when they die?"

"Not if you bury them before they die. Remember all the coal, oil and shale? That's where all the CO_2 went in Earth's early years."

"Yep. And we spent 200 years releasing it again."

I decided to change the subject.

"So have you come across Marco?"

"What, that little slippery jerk? Not a thing. Have you?"

"Yeah. That's why we were down by Beachy Head. We'd followed him down from Midhurst. You may be surprised to know there's a whole wrecked Martian space fleet under the Downs there."

"I'm not surprised at all. They've found their caverns all over the place. They reckon they've been there for hundreds of years waiting for the right moment."

"Did any escape the germ attack?"

"No. Or none we know of. Mind you, they could be manipulating us into thinking they've left. You said when you came back from Helmsley they had some form of telepathy."

"Yes, they did. They've got some sort of third eye which might be something to do with it."

"By the way, Jim. I didn't want to say anything in front of Elizabeth but wasn't she pregnant?"

My relaxed confident mood came to a sudden crash. Wells had mentioned this as well. I had to think fast. We must have arrived at the time line where Elizabeth had come back from Helmsley pregnant. Except, as far as I knew she wasn't.

"Jill. It's complicated. Do you mind not bringing it up with Elizabeth?"

Just then Elizabeth came back from the shower.

--- ~ ---

E.

It was nice to feel clean and to wear garments which were kind to the skin again. When I returned to the parlour, James and Jill were deep in conversation which, to my consternation, stopped when I entered the room.

"Sorry, were you talking about me?"

James looked embarrassed. I cast my mind back wondering what I had done that might have caused offence.

"Yes, we were, Elizabeth. Do you remember what Wells asked you when he spoke on the telephone?"

I cast my mind back and his words about my condition flooded back.

"Yes, I do. He thought I might be with child."

Jill looked at me, at James then back at me.

"I'm sorry, Elizabeth. Jim didn't want me to say anything but as woman to woman I have to know. You remember when you came back from Helmsley you were about six months pregnant. What happened? If you don't mind me asking."

It was true. There was, or is, a time line where I have a child. Oh, this is too much!

--- ~ ---

J.

The time had come to explain to Jill about multiple time lines and multiple persons. That the people she was talking to were actually her brother and sister-in-law but different to the ones she had known before and more importantly she was a different Jill to the one we had left.

It took some time. Not least because we had difficulty dealing with it ourselves.

This Jill thankfully took it on board.

"So, Jim, you and Elizabeth have found that as well as travelling up and down time you are crossing times. Why haven't you met yourselves yet?"

This was a good question. She carried on.

"Imagine being in a room with two of your doppelgangers, dressed in the same clothes. Which partner would you choose, Jim?"

"Both, obviously"

"Good diplomatic answer, Jim, but I'm not convinced you could handle two. What do you think, Elizabeth?"

"If the truth be known, I find often I cannot handle myself let alone another me. Generally, I find just one is more than sufficient in life. However, if such an event did occur we could try some identification that only we would recognise."

"But if they are you they might do the same."

"Then we will just have to tie each other together."

"I can see the merit in that, James, but I also foresee impracticalities."

"You're right. The bath is a bit small for two. But we can save water having a shower."

"You have to give him credit, Elizabeth, for his persistence in trying to get your clothes off."

"I have noticed," said Elizabeth, looking at me, "that men do seem to have inexhaustible funds in this area which is not always matched by its wise expenditure."

I had the distinct feeling that the inadvertent 'groping' in Midhurst may have been alluded to here again. Jill replied.

"Well put, Elizabeth, and I might add that I have also heard that when they do spend, their expenditure is often quicker than one wished."

Much giggling then followed accompanied by an appalling pretence of innocence of the meaning of her remark which I hoped was not entirely at my expense.

Before this conversation disappeared down one of their favourite paths, usually entitled 'Jim and his Hilarious Amorous Adventures,' I changed the subject.

"I know l sound like a broken record, but we need to find Marco. He disappeared in the Mars observatory. We presumed he came this way but he might not have gone through the doors at all."

"Or, James, he has travelled to Midhurst to find his time machine."

This was a good point. This time line had discovered relativity otherwise there would be no GPS. And that meant Maxwell had published his equations. Therefore Midhurst might still have the servers and the time machine controls.

"I think you're right. Looks like we will have to go back there AGAIN! You know I do you feel we are just running round and round in a big circle."

$$--- \sim ---$$

E.

Armed with our candles we entered the St. Mary and St Denys Church again at Midhurst which, although restored to its former self in this world, was now a museum to

66

religious history. It was tastefully done and I felt if a person came here 'looking' for religion they would find the atmosphere agreeable. The tunnel in the crypt was thankfully illuminated by electric lights, but we took our candles, for as James kept on reminding me, you can never have enough candles. The floor was quite clean so we were not able to ascertain for certain that Mr Batalia had visited ahead of us.

When we arrived at the door James pressed it gently with his hand and found it solid and unlocked. It was with some trepidation I entered because I was half expecting to find a copy of myself.

James had tried to reassure me by saying that he thought there was so many time lines it was unlikely such a meeting would ever take place but my imagination was a little too strong to completely agree with him.

The cavern was as we had left it when we despatched Marco to the future. The machinery, I noted was silent, indicating that if Mr Batalia had been here he had been unsuccessful. However we realised we were at an impasse as well.

James said, "So everything is dead and no time machine. One thing though that has just struck me. Is this room on Earth or Mars?"

This was an exceedingly good question, and it encouraged a thought I had been considering on the journey here.

"If it is Mars then are the doors still here?"

We immediately looked around the room. At first there was nothing obvious but James walked over to the walls and proceeded to press his hands point by point along the surface.

To our amazement at three points his hands disappeared into the walls. He then went behind the time control panel where the Earth globe stood motionless in its frame. When he re-emerged he said.

"Elizabeth. Come and see this."

Behind, recessed in the apparatus was a globe of Mars. Unlike the Earth globe, this one was illuminated.

"I think this globe is live. There are small points of coloured light all over it. I wonder if these show the Martian cities. I need a map of Mars."

At this point James removed his phone and quickly tapped some commands.

"Ah. Here it is."

"You have a map of Mars on your phone?"

"Of course, Elizabeth. You never know when it might be needed."

There were times I wondered what went on in James' little world. Jill had said that scientists spend a lot of time 'off planet'. I suspected much of James' off worldliness was spent inside his phone. James had reconnected with his little friend again. In seconds he was tapping away like a small child with a new toy.

"Yes! A map of Mars. Good old ESA. I'll download it."

Within a few moments he was proudly showing me the surface of Mars on his phone.

"Excellent! This one's got all the old Latin names. Look! It's even got the landing sites of Viking, Curiosity, and Opportunity. There's the poor old Beagle!"

I tried to engage with his enthusiasm with limited success for the names were alien to me.

"Let's have a look at what we can match up."

James then went to the Martian globe and began to compare it with his new-found map. He started.

"My God, the landing sites match light points on the globe!"

I confess I had difficulty following his train of thought; eventually after close questioning he informed me these 'landing' sites were where exploration vessels sent by Earth had landed on Mars.

"I understand what you say but I do not see the significance, James."

"I'm not sure myself but I'm struck by the coincidence."

I tried to understand this.

"Then do you think the Martians know of the landing places?"

"If this globe is built by Martians then yes."

"Were they sent by Earth, I mean these vessels, to communicate with the Martians?"

"To communicate with the Martians? Why? You mean the exploration tag was just a cover? Jeez, that would mean.. God, Elizabeth does your brain have an overdrive button? Could Marco and his mates be in league with the Martians? You could be right!"

Unfortunately I was not quite sure what I was 'right' about, let alone whether my mind was subject to this 'overdrive' that he mentioned. James in his imagination had leapt too far for me. I had to catch him and wind him in a little.

"Please, James, your vernacular is confusing me. Do you suggest that there is a link between ComsMesh and the Martians?"

"Yes. But who is controlling who and for what purpose?"

--- ∼ ---

J.

Once again we had to gather together what 'facts' we had and see if anything made sense. Though I suspected as soon as any sense was made another unexpected time driven event would cloud it all again.

Eventually after much discussion in which Elizabeth kept me on the straight and narrow I tried to summarise.

"Try this, Elizabeth. We thought Marco and ComsMesh wanted to socially engineer the world by locking us all in to AdCom. But what was their end goal? Was it purely power? Or was it something else? Was it that they were preparing the Earth to be taken over by the Martians?"

"I can see that is a possibility. But to repeat your question and to add from our discussion with Jill, which, if either, is the puppet master?"

"You mean is ComsMesh controlling the Martians or vice versa. Well, I'm beginning to think the latter. They seem to have the better toys. You know, telepathy, spaceships and some form of time travel."

"And, if you remember Helmsley, that tripod in the castle had been there for hundreds of years. They have been planning an invasion for a long time."

"But why did they wait so long? If they'd done it back in medieval times it would have been a walkover."

"I would agree, James. Which draws one to the conclusion they were waiting for someone or something."

I tried to think what they were waiting for. ComsMesh?

They invaded after we closed down the servers. That removed the social manipulation to make the world compliant.

"Ah! I think I've got it. If they wanted to inhabit our world they needed the right CO_2 atmosphere and the simplest way to do it was to let us do it for them. Remember ComsMesh, in order to manipulate us, was burning up the world's resources by addicting us to more and more material acquisitions and in the process we were releasing CO_2 like there was no tomorrow."

"So, James, their plan was twofold. The first to make the world suitable for them to live in by changing the atmosphere. But, oh, this is difficult to keep all this in my head, but in order to change the atmosphere we had to be scientifically advanced enough. But then we might be able to defend ourselves. I'm running out of fingers, James. Ah! They needed to make us docile so that we couldn't resist them. Does that make sense or have I failed to absorb....."

How did she do it?

I said. "I've decided not to live in your era with you, Elizabeth, because if the men are as bright as you I'll be regarded as a dunce in no time and you will leave me for a man with a brain like yours."

"I'm disappointed to hear that, James, I can assure you the accumulation of knowledge is not the only way to a girl's heart."

"But I'm sure it helps."

"It does, James. But it is its interpretation and application which holds the key and in my experience there are few men who have such skills."

And she reached over and kissed me.

There are times when I'm almost happy.

But back to Mars. How did this Martian globe work?

There were three small controls on the globe which I was sure set the coordinates on the surface. I decided to see if I could move them. I turned the globe so that pointer was over Viking 1. A humming sound filled the room as I turned the globe; when I was over Viking's location it stopped.

I heard Elizabeth whisper, "James!"

"What?"

"Look at the cavern walls."

I turned to where she was looking. The walls had disappeared and in their place was the glass dome we had seen in the previous time line through which we could see the Martian landscape and there in front of us, not more than fifty yards, was Viking 1 sitting on the ground.

"Is that one of your explorers, James?"

"Yes. I just pointed to it on the globe and we've arrived next to it. Let me see the map. Ah yes it landed on the edge of Chrysis Planitae, whatever that means."

"I think she was a minor Greek nymph. It is the plain of the nymph Chryse."

"Oh, nice. Let me try another. I'll try Pathfinder. That's nearby."

I moved the pointer to its position and the humming returned but this time the landscape through the dome rushed past at a tremendous speed across a great rugged plain until the view came to rest besides Pathfinder.

"Wow, we can travel on Mars! Where shall we go?"

$$--- \sim ---$$

E.

James was very excited by his new toy. He spent the next half hour driving all over Mars. In truth, regarding the scenery made me quite dizzy and reminded me not a little of the flying machine we had travelled in before, except in this one we stayed close to the ground. Eventually, thankfully, he tired of his exploits and decided to join me again.

"I hope you haven't woken up the whole of Mars with your reckless driving. I am surprised you haven't attracted the attention of the local constabulary."

"I haven't seen a soul but what I can't figure out is whether this observatory is moving or we are just watching from some mobile camera on a drone or something."

"Perhaps we could try one of those secret doors."

I was about to go to one when James grabbed me rather violently by the arm.

"Stop! If we've actually travelled to these places it could be Mars atmosphere outside!"

"Good God, James! You might have saved my life. I had not thought."

Here was a good example of James' interpretation and application of his knowledge.

"Perhaps we should try a lighted candle?"

He obtained a candle from his knapsack and after lighting it carefully pushed it through the first door. On retrieval it was snuffed out. The second door resulted in the same effect but on the middle door it returned still lit.

"Do you think it is breathable, James?"

"Well, it demonstrates there's quite a bit of oxygen behind there and reasonable pressure."

"So do you think it is safe?"

"I can't remember my chemistry. There might be twenty percent oxygen out there which is good for us. But if there is more than about a few percent of carbon dioxide we will be dead on the first drawn breath."

"Can you look it up, as you say, on your phone?"

"No. That's funny - there's no signal. I know. We could go back and steal a dog or cat. Tie it to my string and send it through."

"James! That is shocking. You will do no such thing! If my sister Flory ever heard of it well... really!"

Then something came into my mind which made me immediately forget about the sacrifice of a small innocent creature.

"Do you think the tunnel back to the church is still there?"

James looked at me then at the door. We walked over to it.

It was at that moment the thought of having a small creature such as a canary to send through first became, I am embarrassed to say, rather attractive.

He slowly opened it. Relief! The tunnel was still there though whether 'out there' was the same time as when we came I did not want to contemplate.

We returned to what to do.

--- ~ ---

J.

If we assumed we were on Mars and we assumed Marco was here then where would he go? We didn't even know what time it was. We didn't really know who he was working for. I returned to the Martian globe and looked more closely at the lights. There were three colours. The red ones I had identified as the Mars landings. That left the blues and the greens. They were all in the mountain regions. Then I had a look at the Mariner Valleys. I had been quite fascinated by it when the first high resolution pictures came back from Mars. It was like a great crack in the landscape and stretched from the three Tharsis volcanoes and the massive dome of Olympus Mons behind. Now that I could see the valley in detail I could see it ran for almost two thousand miles down to the Chrysis Planitae which looked more and more like a sea bed. I was struck by the absence of craters which suggested it was not that geologically old.

By Olympus there was a blue light.

"This Mons Olympus, Elizabeth, I think we'll take a look. It's the highest mountain or volcano on Mars and it commands the whole of the whole Mariner valley down to the plain. I'm also fascinated by those Tharsis Mountains. I hadn't noticed before but look, they're aligned in a straight line almost at right angles to Olympus. It doesn't look natural."

I turned the globe until the pointer was over them. Once again I heard the hidden engines hum. The landscape began to shift and we found ourselves entering the Mariner valley. Mile by mile the cliffs and mountain sides of the valley rose higher and higher towards the sky. I had read that the depth of the valley was greater than Everest and after a while I could believe it. Eventually we began to climb out of the valley and the three Tharsis shield volcanoes, Arsia, Pavonis and Ascraeus Mons appeared on the horizon.

I asked Elizabeth if she knew what their names meant but all she could remember was that Tharsis was a legendary place known in the Bible which was located far across the sea from Israel.

Then as we came out on a lava plain between the three volcanoes with Mount Olympus rising on the horizon, Elizabeth said.

"What are those holes there? Near what did you call it? Mount Arsia?"

I looked where she was pointing and there were seven perfectly circular holes in the surface over five hundred feet in diameter near Arsia Mons. Something was familiar about them. I raked what was left of my brain and then I remembered. The Mars Orbiter had sent back images of holes in the surface around the Tharsis volcanoes. Perfectly circular holes. Now, so much closer, I could see in the weak sunlight they were great caverns reaching deep into the ground. Were these gateways to the Martian world?

--- ~ ---

Chapter Six

J.

I steered the view towards the first cavern. It was big and the walls which descended into blackness were smooth as ice. The three Tharsis volcanoes stood silently in a row before a horizon so strangely close I felt I was just on the edge of the world. Then I remembered Mars was only half the size of Earth. I tried to move closer and down into the hole but the machine resisted. It was then I saw the faint outline of a road or track half covered by the sand stretching before us to the cave.

But as I looked along the track wondering what to do I noticed a small dot appear on it in the distance. It seemed to grow bigger and then bigger! It was coming towards us!

"Jeez! They've spotted us!"

"We must leave, James! Let us go back down the tunnel to safety."

As it got nearer I could see it was a cylindrical gold coloured tube with a smooth conical head at each end. Pipes ran along the sides and the wheels looked like they had been borrowed from a steam engine. In another few moments it reached the observatory and almost filled the screen then stopped motionless. Before I could speak one of the hidden doors in the room began to dissolve.

"Run, James! They are upon us!"

"No. Just wait a second. See what happens. If anything comes out we'll run."

Nothing happened. Elizabeth was pulling very hard on my sleeve. Just a vacant hole in the wall. No rush of air or anything.

I waited for what seemed over a minute with Elizabeth trying to persuade me to run. Still nothing. I made a decision.

"I'm going to have a look."

"Not without me you're not."

We peaked through the door and found we were looking inside the cylinder. It had the air of an art nouveau first class railway carriages with four burgundy upholstered high-backed seats. "This must be a taxi service of some sorts. Perhaps it's automatically despatched when an observatory arrives to take people to the mountain."

"You're not going to go in are you, James? We could be trapped."

Unfortunately, as was later pointed out, once again all reason and sanity escaped me because I decided to enter. Elizabeth reluctantly followed and just as I should have expected the door behind us closed.

"I think we had better take a seat." I said, once we had finished discussing who was the bigger fool and had unanimously agreed that it was me.

--- ~ ---

E.

I am still not completely sure how my advice to escape back to Midhurst resulted in us sitting in an alien carriage with no obvious means of escape as usually I can persuade James by what he calls 'persistent repetition' into agreeing with me. I must admit I cannot completely admonish James because as he sat opposite me, rather dejected, he said he now agreed with my advice wholeheartedly and found no fault in it. Nevertheless his suggestion that perhaps if I had been more 'persistent' in my proposal our situation would have been different was batted back with some vigour.

This tête-à-tête was, however, interrupted and probably for the best, by a sense of motion which conveyed the distinct impression that we were now travelling at speed.

--- ～ ---

J.

The journey took only about five minutes but was long enough considering the topic of conversation. There were no windows, but we sensed the carriage halt by the sudden slow movement of our bodies in the weak gravity. Then the door opened.

We were looking into a large, yellow-lit room. It was distinctly Earth-like. Dials, switches and monitors, connected by cables and pipes filled the walls. Much to our surprise a row of consoles lined the walls, the seats of which were occupied by humans.

When a couple of them turned to see who had arrived the surprise seemed as much on their side. Then an alarm sounded and moments later two more entered by a side door. They seemed disappointed that we didn't have any identification, were not properly dressed for the occasion and our means of arrival were not quite what they expected. This resulted in an invitation to accompany them which we thought best to accept.

--- ～ ---

E.

We were 'escorted' into an hemispherical room lit by the same diffuse yellow light, the origin of which was not obvious. The centre was occupied by a long curved wooden table behind which sat five creatures. Three were of human form, one of whom I immediately recognised. Behind them, the three Tharsis volcanoes shrouded in an orange mist filled a screen which occupied half the room. Our escorts motioned us to sit in front of the table, but we chose to stand. The three humans were engaged in conversation which I could not hear. They did not seem to notice our presence. The two at each end of the table whom I took to be Martian of the type we had seen at Helmsley seemed to be asleep. Eventually the human in the centre turned to us and spoke.

"I am Johann Wundt, Director of the Weber Institute. This is Professor Rollinson, who is the guardian of your diaries and Dr. Batalia, whom I believe you know."

The speaker was a middle-aged man and thin, almost too thin, as though the gravity of Mars had wasted his flesh. He had what James humorously described as an upside-down haircut. Nearly bald on top and a neatly cut, greying beard to compensate.

We did not introduce ourselves, so he continued:

"We believe you are James Urquhart," pointing a thin hand at James and then pointing at me, "and you are either Elizabeth Bicester or Urquhart depending on which time path you have originated from."

I did not let this go.

"In this world, and I hope any other world I travel, I am Elizabeth Urquhart, wife of James Urquhart and that is how you will address me."

My words were followed by a faint rumbling sound which at first I thought was the result of my comment. Then the orange sky behind the volcanoes lit up as though a distant storm was passing. They did not turn round although the two Martians stirred a little before returning to their motionless sleep.

The speaker ignored my remark and continued.

"As you can see, thanks to your interference, the Earth has begun its attack in response to the Martian invasion. Your people have already made most of the surface uninhabitable due to their germ bombs."

Before I could speak James interjected.

"Don't blame us for the mess you're in. We didn't ask to be part of this and, oh yes, I just remembered. Mars attacked us first."

"Yes, that is a problem. We had hoped to find a way to restart the servers first. But the number of future lines of opportunity was diminishing rapidly."

His last words were a surprise and of some importance to me. I had thought that there were an infinite number of futures but if I understood him correctly his reply suggested that not all futures were stable and, more importantly, futures were disappearing. I decided to explore this thought later with James if I had the opportunity. But I had sensed a weakness which needed exploiting and goaded them by saying:

"Mr Wundt, if I have pronounced your name correctly, do you mean that every time you attempt to start your infernal machines, we are there to stop you?"

"Yes, your doppelgangers are always there."

"Maybe that is telling you something about human resistance to manipulation, Mr Wundt."

He did not take kindly to this.

"You realise that men AND women in their quest for knowledge or greed can be persuaded to do just about anything, given the right type of stimulation, Mrs Urquhart?"

He glanced rather pointedly at the two Martians.

As I tried to absorb the possible implications of his statement, which sounded like a threat, James replied with a new thread of enquiry.

"Just a minute. I've heard something like that before. In fact I've heard your name before! Didn't you have an ancestor who believed that Man was, what was it, ah yes, without spirit and was nothing more than just the sum of his experiences and stimuli? You know like an insect or perhaps those two Martians there pretending to be asleep."

Despite James' reference to the two alien creatures they remained motionless.

Mr Wundt said. "You are well read, Mr Urquhart."

"No, I'm not, and my wife will vouch for that. I just like to keep abreast of the people who try to control history. It helps me decide when politicians and megalomaniacs are lying."

I should confess that once upon a time I regarded James as not as savoir faire in some areas as I wished. This was especially true in the classics where in certain company his ignorance was often embarrassingly apparent.

I had been conditioned to respect those who could speak fluent Greek and Latin and were able to quote from the bible just by referring to the verse numbers. Until I met James I confess I had looked up to these people. However, he showed me through example, with certain notable and inexplicable exceptions to which I will not refer as they do not lend weight to my argument, that the accumulation of knowledge for knowledge's sake without application was an empty vessel and eventually led to a closed, comfortable world where progress was nil. Like the vicar in a village where no one could read or write and who fed them solely on the scriptures for their comfort while they fell sick and died for want of some simple sanitation. Or the eastern philosopher Al-Ghazali who with one stroke of his philosophy closed the minds of the Arabic renaissance for hundreds of years.

I could see Mr Wundt was having difficulty with James' remark. A conversation ensued between the three humans, which concluded when Mr Batalia spoke up.

"The problem we have, Urquhart, is that your continued presence is preventing the natural flow of time from allowing us to achieve our end goal."

"No, the problem you've got," replied James, "is that we are preventing you from turning my world into a land of docile sheep so that your Martian friends can take it over."

This was an arrow well shot for I noticed the Martian on the left open its eyes. I felt myself drawn to its rabbit-like visage until I remembered its effect at Helmsley. I tried to look away quickly, but it was too late. I felt it join my mind.

The room slowly vanished like treacle running down a glass pane revealing a strange, almost Earth-like, landscape. The sky was no longer orange but dark blue and the plains had become seas. Impossibly high waves rolled in lines across to the horizon and fell in slow motion against the shores. The scene dissolved and reappeared but this time, mountains began to rise like bubbles in boiling oil which, to my horror, burst, showering the land with thick smoke and lava. Then another vision: great rents opened in the surface and the seas began to tumble into them cascading down chasms into the bowels of the planet. The water receded from the shores until all that was left were a few pools in the dry plains. Once again the scene changed. The land had turned red and the sky an almost opaque misty orange. It was the world we saw now. I do not know how long this catastrophe took. It may have been thousands of years or just decades but it changed their world for ever.

As I dwelt on this thought I felt my mind focus on a point of light in the sky. It slowly expanded until it was blue. Another planet smaller than the first rotated round it. It expanded until I could see the Earth in all its glory with its mighty oceans. A feeling of yearning percolated through me for the want of water but as I involuntarily reached for that watery world the apparition dissolved and I was returned to the room to find to my astonishment James being held quite firmly between our two escorts.

--- ~ ---

J.

I saw the creature open its eyes and look at Elizabeth but before I could do anything she was already in a trance. I leapt for the Martian. Unfortunately I had momentarily forgotten the effect of Newton's Laws of Motion in the weak Martian gravity and to my consternation I flew, or should I say slid, headfirst over the table right past the creature and only succeeded in hitting it with my arm. However, I discovered Mr Newton's laws also seems to apply to the Martian who, due to its much lighter weight, was propelled upwards at some rate and ricocheted off the ceiling before returning to the table, bouncing and then sliding into Wundt's lap. I, on the other hand, demonstrated a change of momentum from the contact by spinning round and knocking Marco to the floor. Our escorts unfortunately had a much better grasp of equal and opposite reaction and were upon me before I got to my senses.

They dragged me back to Elizabeth. This time our escorts stood right next to us. Wundt and Marco quickly recomposed themselves. However the Martian had become distinctly animated and gave the impression that it wasn't completely happy with its human friends who, judging by the contorted expressions on their faces, seemed to be locked in a mind battle with it.

Eventually it calmed down. Marco wrenched himself out of whatever dream state he had been in and turning to me said: "We're going to start the servers. Follow me."

Before I could say anything the wall to the left dissolved and they took us rather unwillingly into another room. Before us were rows of screens: some blank, others showing what looked like the cavern at Midhurst, although I couldn't be sure as although they looked similar they were not quite. The time machine controllers only appeared in five of them. In others the cavern was empty. In front of the screens were groups of dials and controls operated by half a dozen Martians. Every now and then a screen would go blank before starting up again but with the image fainter than before. I realised what they were. They were futures. The Martians were able to see the future!

--- ~ ---

Chapter Seven

J.

We stood staring at the screens. Our escorts stood very close to us on either side. Wundt turned to us and said:

"In case you haven't guessed you are looking at the present in the futures we can see. The blank screens are where the time lines are either closed or inaccessible to us. Yes, and before you ask the Martians are able to slide across time. As you can see there are just five futures where the time controllers and servers still exist but they are all shut down"

"What a shame. Can't you find a time line where the servers are working?"

"All those that were have been shut down by you."

"I hadn't realised we were so good at our job, Elizabeth."

"I must admit there were times when the goals of our devious plans were not completely apparent to me either."

I turned to Marco.

"So why don't you get your time transponder and think your way back in time, wait for us and carry us off?"

"Because those time lines are closed."

"Do you mean they are just closed to your Martian friends? Just because you can't see them doesn't mean they don't exist."

"Maybe they do but it's irrelevant because they are inaccessible."

A plan was forming in my head. Marco hadn't denied he had the transponder. What would happen if we got hold of the time transponder that Marco had used to escape? I carried on.

"So why are these futures closed?" I pointed at the blank screens.

"Because they can't exist. We believe for a time line to exist there must be logical continuity. Remember, time like space is a dimension with a certain length. Each point must logically lead to the next point. If it doesn't then the time line stops. The future stops there. Those blank screens are where the time line has already stopped in the past."

"And the futures which exist now - how do you know they won't suddenly stop?"

"We don't. But we do believe that soon there may be only one future. "

I began to understand. The number of possible futures was diminishing. If they could get the servers working then perhaps all the time lines would coalesce into the one where ComsMesh takes over the world. There was also Marco's time machine sitting dormant in 2016. Then I woke up. It was nearly 2016! All we had to do was get back to Chichester, wait a few days, pop up to Midhurst and find a way to start the time machine. I'll get Elizabeth to fill in the details with one of her spiffing plans. Simple really. But first I had to find out what Marco was up to.

"So how are you going to start them up?"

"You are."

"Excellent. When are we going?"

I might have overplayed my enthusiasm as the three humans now looked very confused and suspicious. Elizabeth wasn't too happy either.

Marco said "What are you playing at, Urquhart?"

I drew Elizabeth close and said, "We just want to go home."

---~---

E.

Up to this point I had thought James and I were as one. However his sudden willingness to assist them with their plans confused me somewhat. I feared one of his inexplicable brainstorms had taken hold again. However, he looked very calm and signalled he had a plan by putting his arm round me and gently pinched me on the waist in the manner I had done to him in Midhurst and NOT in the way he had 'handled' me previously.

We were escorted back to the carriage. Mr Rolllinson and Mr Batalia joined us. The five-minute journey to the observatory was spent in silence though not without regard for each other. When we arrived Mr Batalia alighted first, and Mr Rollinson motioned us to follow which we did though not without consternation.

Mr Batalia went immediately to the machine and adjusted a lever on the globe to take us back to the Chryse Planatae.

While he 'drove' the device I noticed that Mr Rollinson was watching Mr Batalia like a hawk. He gave the distinct impression that he did not trust him any more than we did.

Then the view of Mars shivered and vanished leaving the blank cavern walls we had found when we first entered. We were back on Earth and there in its cradle was the black shape of Mr Batalia's time machine. It was 2016.

I had a sudden impulse to run out of the cavern and back to Midhurst while Mr. Batalia was distracted, but I resisted mainly because I didn't know where to run to but more importantly I had no idea where James stood in this situation.

Mr Batalia turned. "Perfect!" he said with a smile that indicated he was pleased with himself, "And a bonus, my time machine. Once the Servers are up and running I'll have that as well and be out of here."

However, I noticed that Mr Rollinson was not totally in agreement, judging by the antique revolver he had produced from his pocket and was now pointing in the general direction of Mr Batalia.

"I'm afraid, Mr Batalia, that your work is finished here now. I am returning you to Mars."

He then by means of the weapon persuaded Mr Batalia whom I could see was not completely happy with the situation to pass through the door which we had previously found had kept the candle lit.

I made a note that the air behind that door was either breathable or Mr Batalia had met a rather unpleasant end. I hoped it was the former for I did not want to discover that Mr Rollinson was capable of cold-blooded murder.

He then turned to us.

It was the first time I had regarded Mr Rollinson properly. Like Mr Wundt he was of a certain age and sported a similar grey beard. However, unlike Mr Wundt he seemed to have benefitted from a generous regime. He was wearing a tweed jacket, green corduroy trousers and tooled leather brown shoes. He also smelled of tobacco. It was then that I noticed the shirt. It carried a winged collar. I should have noticed earlier but in my time this was commonplace.

"Before we begin I would like to thank you for your diaries. You do realise if you hadn't written them we would never had discovered you and time travel and set up ComsMesh."

Before responding I thought I would explore his background a little as I have often found an unexpected deviation from a topic advantageous in winning an argument. James on occasion had commented that he thought women were particularly adept at this when a discussion was not going in their favour. I, of course, could not possibly comment.

"Mr Rollinson...."

"It is Rolleston, Madam."

He then spelt it for me so there would be no doubt. His accent was familiar and of my class but I could not quite place it.

"Pray forgive me, Mr Rolleston, but I could not help but notice your clothes."

"Because?"

"Pardon, but they do seem to be of a fashion not greatly different from the world in which I lived."

"You are quite astute. Then you may have heard of my reputation. I founded the Irish Literary Society of 1891.

"I am afraid not, sir. It is a little after my time."

I had now placed the accent but before I could enquire further James interjected with some excitement.

"My God! Are you T. W. Rolleston, the chap who wrote that stuff on Celtic legends?"

"You are correct. Sir, I am flattered I am still known in your time."

"I have one of your books. Published by Harrap, I think."

"Ah yes, that was very popular at the turn of the last century. But there was much competition with Mr Yeats and his circle with whom I did not always see eye to eye."

As I have written before, I had thought James was not famous for his literary knowledge but maybe I had misjudged him. Perhaps he had areas which were just not topical in my circle. I tried a little test of the Celtic literary groups I had known.

"Do you know of Lady Charlotte Guest or George MacDonald, James?"

"Not personally but yes, she translated 'The Mabinogion'. One of my favourite books and MacDonald wrote that fairy book 'The Phantastes'."

It was as though I had lit a small candle in his mind. I must explore this further. Perhaps we should prepare and exchange a list of our favourite books. But James had returned the conversation back to Mr Rolleston and away from my deviation.

"So how are you going to start the machinery?"

"I'm not."

This somewhat surprised us. He continued:

"In fact, I've no intention of starting the system again."

$$--- \sim ---$$

J.

The shock of meeting T.W. Rolleston made me almost miss what he said. I fired questions at him rapidly. What was he doing here in this time? Why didn't he want the servers started? And what about the Martians? And I nearly forgot the most important one, what was he going to do with us? For I noticed he was still holding the weapon.

"Let me take your questions in reverse order. First, I intend you both no harm providing you do not attempt to start that machinery."

And by way of reassurance he returned the weapon to his pocket.

"Second, the Martians have been here on Earth for a long time, thousands of years in fact."

"If that's the case then where are they? Don't tell me they're walking the streets masquerading as humans. I've seen that film."

"No, they are not but their presence has been detected many times. Legends are full of their exploits."

"Are you saying they are the fairies, the Sidhe and the goblins?"

"Yes. That is exactly what they are. They first arrived in the Mesolithic period."

I tried to think what was going on back then. It was when Britain was still joined to the continent via Doggerland in the North Sea. I remembered that it was also when those delicate tiny flint arrows first appeared which until archaeologists proved otherwise people associated with the fairy folk. Was Rolleston saying they were Martians?

"So where can we find these fairies?"

"Their locations are in plain sight. You know them as the long barrows and cairns you see across the hills of Western Europe."

"But those are burial chambers. Most of those excavated have human remains in them."

"Yes, humans have been buried in them. They hoped to be transported to the other world. But they were initially built as portals. I am sure you have read that in Celtic legends. They are not without substance. They have come down to us through hundreds of generations. These barrows are the entrances to that familiar place of our dreams, the "Other World."

"You mean like New Grange, West Kennet, Hetty Peglars Tump? But I've visited loads of these places and seen nothing."

"How do you know? How do you know the world when you entered was the same as the world when you came out?"

"Well, it looked the same. All my friends seemed the same."

"But was it you who came out or just another version of you?"

I began to understand. We had been going in and out of portals and finding ourselves in different futures every time.

"So these places are portals by which the Martians visit this planet?"

"And by which we can visit theirs."

"So why don't they join us? We are in a more enlightened time now. I'm sure we wouldn't try and kill them if they were friendly."

"They are not human. They are totally different in morals, ethics and thought. They have telepathy of sorts and also more importantly they have the ability to choose a limited number of futures."

"So they know what the futures are going to bring and choose the best one? That must give you a whole new outlook on life."

"Not quite. They can only see a little way and the number of futures they see change."

"That's what we saw on those screens on Mars?"

"I believe so. They were designed by the Martians to allow us to see a little as they do. From what I understand the really big difference between us and them is that we are constrained by our four-dimensional world. They on the other hand partially occupy a fifth dimension. This allows them to 'see' the time dimension they travel on and alter it a little."

"So what we really saw on those screens was them manipulating time futures."

"No, they bend the lines and see if it continues to exist. The blank screens are those where a future line doesn't hold."

"And basically they can't bend the future enough to get the servers working?"

"That's right."

"But I thought this was a future where there was a possibility."

"Yes. But as you've just seen it hasn't happened."

"So what are the Martians going to do now? What do they want?"

"Do not worry. That is not your concern anymore."

"Oh yes, it is. They need our world, or more importantly, they need our water"

"I do not think so. This world will soon not have enough water. The atmosphere is already changing. You have seen how hot it is."

"But Earth is dealing with it."

"Do you think so? I doubt they will have enough time. Other gases are releasing. The permafrost is melting giving off great quantities of methane that will trap the solar heat. You are too close to the sun. The temperature in space in the sunlight is over 100C. The seas will boil off."

"So this world is doomed!"

"Yes. Your only hope is to colonise Mars. You possibly have a hundred years to terraform it and now you have the Martian technology from their invasion to do it."

"And you made sure the servers were kept shut down to give us time!"

"That is correct. I wish you luck."

"Pardon?"

"You can go home."

"What, just leave? The way we came in?"

"Yes. You can forget all about us. I think the last opportunity to start the machines is gone. Goodbye."

And with that he went through the door he'd sent Marco.
We stood there alone in the cavern
"So what do we do now, James?"
"Take his advice."

___~___

E.

James opened the door to the tunnel.

"Oh dear, it looks like we need the candles. Where or when the hell are we now?"

We lit them and walked along until we came to the corridor to the crypt.

"Elizabeth! I think I can hear singing."

I listened. He was right. It sounded like a choir practice. We quietly went up to the door. It became louder. I recognised the practice of an evensong.

I was just about to open the door when James suggested a peep through the keyhole might be more prudent. I bent down and looked through. He was right. There was half a dozen ladies and gentleman singing from hymn books and dressed in the fashion of my time. Somehow we had returned to the nineteenth century. If this was not worrying enough I realised I was dressed in the fashion of James' era which although quite modest for his time, would have me arrested as a strumpet if I appeared in the church and streets here. Sometimes I do feel that men impose rather unnecessary restrictions on women. I can only conclude it is for their benefit and not ours for I have not found a change of fashion has changed greatly my moral outlook. But maybe that says something about my moral fibre. I will leave that there for my moral integrity was about to be challenged in a different and more serious way, for James' solution to this problem of clothing involved 'borrowing' overcoats from the vestry when the choristers had returned to the nave. This was beyond the pale even by James' standards and I am afraid to say I admonished him quite severely for his suggestion. He agreed with me entirely that seeing a broadsheet with an article regarding a lady of reasonable means arrested and taken to the circuit judge for stealing clothes from good parishioners in a church would banish her from acceptable society for ever. And he also accepted that it would place an unbearable stigma on her family necessitating them packing up post haste and moving 'up North' to a God forsaken town in the Potteries where the colour of their character would quickly blend with their surrounds.

I should also note that what he thought was a generous offer to 'look after me' if such a brush with the law occurred was not well received either.

Which makes it rather difficult to admit, I am rather appalled to say, and it was a measure of our situation, that I eventually acquiesced to his proposal! For I could see no other solution. If anyone ever reads this and comments on my momentary moral dereliction my only defence or excuse was a fear of being seen half-naked so to speak.

Though on second thoughts if these diaries were made public in court I imagine I would be regarded as a mad women and locked up in Bedlam immediately!

And so to the crime. We waited for about half an hour in the tunnel like two felons who felt they were going to be "fingered" as Mr Dickens says. Then when the singing stopped, and the crypt was quiet we opened the door. Seeing no one we quietly walked on tiptoe to the vestry where I 'acquired' a plain burgundy overcoat and James a brown one. I had now done the crime. I swear if anyone had entered at the moment the guilt on our faces would have led them quickly to the conclusion we were lifting the church silver!

James later said he was so scared by our actions that if we had been accused of stealing the silver and the lead off the roof he would have confessed to them as well.

Unfortunately in planning our crime I realised we had not planned a means of escape. I should record a little panic arose at that moment which brought not a few tears to my eyes.

There were only two opportunities. The first to walk through the church and possibly meet the owners of the coats where we would attempt to discuss jocularly how common was the fashion for brown and burgundy. The second was to continue to the inn where we might find our room occupied and have to try to explain to the occupants how we had lost our way and were as surprised as they were. Neither of these plans felt safe. Nor did James help to placate me by saying that after stealing the coats, silver and roof lead, a little bit of burglary would not add a great deal to our sentence. And besides, he added, I should not worry too much as he had been to Australia and found the convicts quite friendly.

Sometimes I do worry about how James deals with adversity.

$$--- \sim ---$$

J.

We decided to go back to the inn. Luckily there was no one in the chamber so we went out through the door and down the stairs to the bar. It was quite crowded, and the smell of pie made me almost ravenous but we couldn't afford to be recognised. Unluckily we were spotted by the innkeeper as we tried to make for the exit.

"Hello again, Sir, Madam. Have you enjoyed your stay here?"

Oh, what would I give for a stable time world?

"Yes, we did, thank you very much." I replied trying to figure out where and when we'd been. And then I remembered just in time.

"How much do we owe you for the lodgings?"

"Nothing, sir. That is all paid for by Mr Wells. He intimated you are well known for your comings and goings and, how can I say, sometimes forgetful in your obligations and he quite generously ensured everything would be alright."

"I must thank him. Is he in town?"

"I believe he is in London."

I had hoped he was in Midhurst because it would have made a perfect bolt hole and also may have answered a lot of questions.

We went out into the street. The sun was high in the east indicating mid-morning. I checked my watch. It said half past four. However, the church clock said ten thirty and so in the absence of anything else to tell me the time I decided to adjust the watch hands to that of the church.

As we wondered what to do next I spotted a paper boy and glancing at the sheets found it was 1873, the year I first met Elizabeth. So much for Rolleston sending me home. We decided to leave town. I would have preferred the train but Elizabeth convinced me that the sooner we left the better and persuaded me to take a cab or bone-shaker, as I called it, to Cocking which she thought would be sufficiently remote from anyone she knew. On arriving we found a pub and treated ourselves to a well-earned three courser. After we had finished I said:

"So, Elizabeth, what shall we do now?"

"It's time for you to meet my father."

"What!"

"You will like him, James. He is quite witty for his age and has the tolerance of a father who has two daughters."

"Or the intolerance of a father who jealously guards his daughters from all suitors."

"We will have to see. I'm sure when you explain how you led his daughter into a life of crime he will be quite receptive."

"That's not fair. I don't remember you coming up with anything better."

"I know, James", she said, holding my hand and then with that melting smile of hers, "We do have fun, do we not, James? And afterwards I always say I would not have missed it for the world. Now, drink up, it is time to meet him."

$$---\sim---$$

Chapter Eight

J.

We managed to persuade a hackney carriage returning from Chichester to take us to Hamgreen. This allowed me to be introduced to the B roads of the nineteenth century which as far as I could tell were any routes where sufficient trees had been removed to allow a carriage to pass. Having spent a lot of time walking on the downs in my era without ever seeing anyone I was surprised by the number of people out working. I had always thought farm work consisted mainly of ploughing, husbandry, crop growing and harvesting. But here I could see much of the labour was utilised in a battle against nature. All along our journey people were working hard on clearing roads, mending fences and cleaning ditches. I made a mental note that when I got back to my own time I would pay more attention to the work they had done. When we arrived much shaken and paid off the driver we approached the main entrance. On each visit to Elizabeth's house I had found its appearance fascinating. On first impression it looked like a typical Georgian lodge with ashlar wall. But here and there were arched windows and a heavy stone buttress on the east side suggested the place was much older. The round wooden studded entrance door however was distinctly medieval and out of place and I often wondered why it was not removed when it had its Georgian makeover. The door opened and an elderly man in an embroidered dressing gown and round flat velvet Turkish cap complete with tassel hat appeared. Elizabeth immediately ran to him.

"Father!"

"Lizzy! You are home. I have only just returned myself."

I made a note of her nickname for future use.

"I did not know you had been away!"

"Business in Bombay again. I took a packet via the Suez Canal. It saved a fortnight I am sure though we made slow progress in the Mediterranean. But, anyway, I hear you have been travelling yourself and married as well. You have been busy. But where is your new husband your sister was telling me about?"

"He is here, father."

I must admit after looking at my clothes he recovered well.

"Good afternoon, Mr Urquhart. I hope you find my daughter manageable?"

"Father!"

Brilliant character assessment. However, I suppressed the devil in me to join in until I knew him better. First impressions are always important.

"She is a joy to be with, Sir."

I suddenly realised I didn't know what to call him.

"Well, Lizzy, you have an interesting catch from what I hear. Now do come in and have some tea."

An old footman arrived to take our coats. I felt a little underdressed looking at his immaculate stiff white shirt and buttoned waist coat. Elizabeth immediately made an excuse to go upstairs and change.

"Please let me change first, father. My clothes are much worn from travelling and I could do with refreshment. Take James into the salon and ask him to tell you all about our adventures. I'm sure you will be surprised with what he has been doing."

The floor below me fell away. I looked at Elizabeth who I swear had an impish grin on her face.

I was going to be left alone with a Victorian father-in-law.

"Well, Mr Urquhart, or may I call you James? Come and have a small snifter while Lizzy is away. I find it is very medicinal after a long journey. By the way my hearing is not what it was so you will have to speak up."

Life was getting better.

We went into the salon, and he motioned me to an armchair then went to a sideboard loaded with decanters and soda dispensers and poured about three inches of whisky in to a crystal glass. As I looked at it I wondered how much I was going to give away by the time I'd finished it. I thought I'd get in first.

"So Sir, if you don't mind me asking, where have you been on your travels?"

"I have been to India. As you no doubt know since the 1870 War there has been much turmoil in the world. The price of iron and cotton has halved and the monies extracted by the new Germany from France has created a power house in the German unified states. They are greatly improving their infrastructure and flooding the market with cheap iron and steel."

I hoped the war he was talking about was the Franco-Prussian War.

"I would have thought with the Suez Canal open it would be advantageous to Britain with shorter trade routes and, I would have hoped, cheaper products from the East"

"There is some merit in what you say but it has removed the need for many of the coaling stations and ports around Africa and they are in decline and require support."

We then talked a little on the demise of transport in the southern hemisphere at the end of which I noticed I had inexplicably emptied my glass. He noticed as well.

"Have another snifter, James, and pray tell me as a new member of the family what would you advise to remove this depression our country has entered?"

I tried to remember anything I could on Victorian economics and politics and sadly came up with little and certainly nothing on what might be a sound investment. My only hope was to be suitably vague but also earn respect as the husband of his daughter.

Then as I picked up my glass refilled with another generous three fingers there was the sound of something hitting the floor above. I looked up.

"Ignore that, James. It will be Lilly preparing the bedrooms. She is a little frail and sometimes drops things. Most of the time we keep the family heirlooms out of her reach. But back to my question."

"I have limited knowledge in this area, Sir. I only read the broadsheets and I hope you agree, their editorials at best only reflect the whim of their owners."

"Absolutely, Sir, they are the last place to find knowledge but the first to find what the public will be told to think tomorrow; thus, sadly for guarding one's investments, they are required reading." No change there then in the last hundred years I thought.

"But your view, James. What is it? For I do not have much opportunity to listen to your generation."

It was time to jump in the pond.

"If pressed then my view is that of Mr Keynes whom I have read."

I could see he expected more so I continued,

"Societies which have a degree of laissez faire and depend on trade are subject to fluctuations in their wealth. I am sure you know there are regular ups and downs in our economy for which our politicians claim responsibilities for the 'ups' and blame others for the 'downs'."

He nodded in agreement. "It is almost a requirement to be a successful politician." Encouraged I took another wee dram and continued.

"My opinion is that when times are good then taxes should rise and governments should put money away for the rainy day which surely comes as day follows night. But when that day comes the government should spend their savings from the good times on infrastructure, for example, roads and railways thereby creating employment, implementing new technology and improving the skills of the work force."

"And thereby be ready for the next upturn. A good proposal, James. I had forgotten the optimism of youth and its simplification of matters."

"I'm sorry, Sir. I did not mean to be so naive."

"Do not take offence, young man. I did not mean that. I was purely reminding myself that although experience is a necessary requirement to the success of any project, too much can also be a great inhibitor. Your theory though would require some improvement in human nature. I have found unfortunately that in the good times everybody wants to leap on the band wagon but when it is bad then money vanishes and everyone becomes unaccountably prudent."

There was only about a quarter of an inch of whisky in my glass when Elizabeth appeared. She looked ravishing. A beautifully embroidered red dress which just failed to cover her shoes and a small bustle which nicely emphasised her bottom. Her neck was bare and she had managed to put a few ringlets in her hair.

"Hello, Father" she said, coming over to kiss him on the head then noticing me and my glass.

"I see you have been softening up my poor husband with one of your malts. I hope you have not extracted too many secrets."

"He has done very well, Lizzy. I think he is a man who can hold his own though I would be interested to know who your tailor is; and come to think if it, where did you buy your cloak?"

We both involuntarily looked at each other which was noticed by her father who rather diplomatically said:

"I see that is subject which we can possibly delay until dinner and a more convivial atmosphere when Flory arrives from Billinghurst. In the meantime, James, I hear you are a star gazer and according to Flory you have expounded interesting theories on the universe. After dinner would you like to see my optics? I have a small observatory at the back of the house where one can find a little solitude."

I suspected that someone's sister had filled in a lot of detail already and knowing her she had carefully sown a few traps for me. It would be best not to deviate too far from the truth.

--- ～ ---

E.

On arriving at my rooms I found my old maid, Lilly, was freshening my bed.

"Hello, Miss, I saw you arrive and I thought I would make your rooms a little more welcoming."

She was a lovely old lady who had been with the family since before I was born. Her only fault was that she knew me too well.

"Thank you, Lilly, and it is good to see you again."

"I have only made up one bed. Will that be sufficient?"

A simple question from which much would be drawn from the answer and embellished in its retelling.

"That will be perfect, Lilly."

"I'm glad. It saves me making up two chambers. But I must warn you that the springs are not what they are and are apt to squeak if put upon too heavily." She said with a knowing grin and hoping for extra spice for the downstairs tea table.

"I do not know what you mean, Lilly." Giving just enough meaning in my answer to satisfy the most inquisitive servant.

"And nor do I at my age, I am sure."

I made the mistake of removing my coat revealing in the process my grey blouse and short skirt. I only noticed this when Lilly dropped a warming pan.

I apologised quickly with a very weak excuse.

"I'm sorry, Lilly, we had an accident with the cab. And being rather muddy our friends lent us some clothes."

I realised now that my chance of entering heaven was almost non-existent.

"But what are those garments? They look like they were made by a rag-a-muffin who, by the looks of it, ran out of cloth before it was finished. I've never seen the likes, Miss Lizzy. I am surprised your husband didn't rush you into a shop to protect your modesty!"

"We were in a difficult situation, Lilly, and I insisted we came straight home. Please do not tell Father. He will worry so!"

"Well, what's done is done. Now let's get you dressed so you are respectable."

Before I could stop her she removed my coat and proceeded as habit to undo my blouse. Her eyes nearly popped out of her head, poor dear, when she saw my bra. It was one which, I should say, James found favourable.

"Well I never, Lizzy! What is this? Have you injured your chest and in need of support?"

"It is a new device that has become popular in the Alps to assist ladies when involved in strenuous exercise such as riding and walking."

I did not know where I was going with this nor how it had entered my head. I can only think it was due to long exposure to James.

She looked at it curiously then demolished my weak reply.

"Poppycock, Miss Lizzy. By its embroidery and colours, I would say it was more likely to find use in a bordello then on a mountain pass."

"I would not know, Lilly. I do not frequent such places."

"And nor do I but if I did I'd imagine such things would be found there. Did your husband buy you this?"

I was cornered.

"He is quite favourable to my wearing them."

"I can see he would be. And I might add I could see such garments becoming quickly fashionable at debutantes' balls. At any road, let's get you into a corset and dressed."

"I am not going to wear a corset, Lilly."

"Suit yourself, Miss Lizzy, I know you well enough to know you're not for persuading but mark my words you will be commented on."

It took some time to be dressed to Lilly's satisfaction, but I was pleased with the result. Though how all this will be retold in the servants' room I dread to think.

When I arrived downstairs my father and James were discoursing quite convivially which I quickly noticed was being oiled with the aid of father's malt.

--- ~ ---

J.

It was remarked on a number of occasions that my clothes were not suitable for dinner, and I was eventually escorted upstairs to a dressing room where a range of suits owned by her father were available. After about half an hour I managed to fit into something that didn't make me look like one of the Marx Brothers.

When Elizabeth saw me she said she now understood why I referred to gentlemen's formal evening wear as 'monkey suits' and I should be prepared for an interesting time with her sister when she arrived.

This interesting time came very soon.

Flory was a picture of a Victorian winter chocolate box. Thankfully she recognised me immediately for I couldn't cope with another time path.

"James, it is so nice to see you again, but I see by your dress you have taken up tailoring. Has your wife abandoned her duties?"

In order to get the suit to fit I had gathered in material and sewn it together. Not very successfully, I might add.

"Luckily I did not marry her for her sewing or her culinary skills", quickly adding for diplomacy sake, "though I am sure if called upon she will manage admirably."

One to me. Seeing no further sport there she then turned to Elizabeth.

"You are looking well, Elizabeth, and I might say, regarding your waist, you are enjoying a relaxed regime."

"I'm enjoying not wearing a corset."

Judging by Flory's face, admitting this in mixed company seemed to be the equivalent of turning up starkers at a wake.

I thought I'd join in to set the evening.

"It's my fault, Flory. I'm not very good at untying knots."

Unfortunately I had misinterpreted the reason for Flory's look. For their father had come into the room and was standing behind us. His partial deafness saved us.

"Ahh! Flory. Did I hear you were tying the knot? Who is the lucky fellow? Is it that young Freddie you met at the theatre in Chichester?"

"I am not 'tying a knot' as you say with anyone, Father. And by the bye Frederick is just a good friend!"

I was going to get on with this chap very well. I was just about to explore the Flory-Freddie relationship when the dinner gong sounded. Saved by the bell.

I like Victorian dinners. They're like Christmas but with more port.

--- ~ ---

E.

Dinner went very well until Flory who sensed the conversation turning to her romances and deflected it towards James.

"James, I'm sure our father would like to hear the latest developments on our stellar and planetary firmament. Can you expound on that 'new clear' theory of yours?"

I remembered last time James tried to expound on his nuclear mechanism of the birth of the sun to my friends, it did not go well.

"Why yes, Mr Urquhart? Flory here has told me about your wondrous tales of star formation. Geologists are now telling us that the Earth is far older than Bishop Usher's calculations and although I have read that even if the sun were made of coal and would burn up within 50,000 years it is said that the Earth may be millions of years of years older. Thus the earth was made before the sun. A certain Professor Helmholtz has tried to resolve this conundrum by postulating that it is the weight of gravity that compresses the sun and the atoms are pressed together so tightly that the friction causes heat and light. If such a mechanism could occur the sun would last a million years".

I looked at James and then at the large glass in his hand.

"It is a good theory, sir, but some scientists have now said the heat is so great at the centre that the atoms themselves fuse together. Hydrogen becomes helium becomes carbon, etc. and in the process give off huge amounts of energy. Such a mechanism it is said could last billions of years making the sun far older than the Earth."

"A million million years?"

"No, I meant a thousand million years. Some scientists, mainly our colonial cousins, have forgotten what the 'bi' means in a billion".

"That is an interesting theory as that would allow the sun to create the Earth. But it has a whiff of transmutation of the elements. Silver turned into gold if you know what I mean. I must warn you," he said jocularly, " that in the wilder parts of Sussex, and by that I mean near the cathedral cloisters, burning at the stake might be suggested for believing in such things as alchemy."

"It is a problem with science that the more is discovered the further God and heaven move away."

This was dry and dangerous ground which could ignite the question of belief but my father, whom I sometimes suspected of having agnostic tendencies started to put God back into his rightful place.

"There is some truth in that. And science must be careful not to reach the conclusion I think you are intimating, suffice to say I believe, that all that science is doing is discovering God's secrets and they are there for the taking."

Flory saw the path this was taking and pushed it further, directing a question at James.

"Do you think that science will prove that God does not exist one day, James?"

I prayed James would not take an atheist line.

"Every time we solve a mystery of the universe we find some new mystery and one would be a fool not to wonder what other secrets its maker is waiting to show us."

Relief. James had made a perfect reply.

$$--- \sim ---$$

J.

After an excellent dinner and already feeling slightly the worse for wear after three glasses of whisky, followed by the wine and port I was invited to see Elizabeth's father's 'optics'. His observatory was really a conservatory in which by means of screws he could open the roof glass. He had all the toys I had ever wanted. Brass astrolabes, a clock-work orrery and two telescopes, one of which was of the nautical Newtonian variety and the other a 10-inch reflector!

But of more interest was the three-foot diameter globe of Mars complete with the 'canals' painted on the surface. I immediately walked or should I say staggered over to it.

"Ah, you like my Martian globe, James. It was bequeathed to me a few years ago by my dear old friend Mr William Dawes. Sadly he is now dead. But he had an eagle eye for the stars. He did some drawings for Mr Proctor, a fellow of the Royal Astronomical Society who like you has an interest in the heavens. Have you heard of him?"

"Yes, I have. The drawing became popular in my circles."

"Well, Old Eagle Eye fashioned a globe based on his drawings and when he died I found I was the benefactor."

A thought came into my sodden brain.

"Have you seen the surface yourself, Sir? I imagine this reflector might do the job."

"Yes, I have. Do you want to have a look? Mars is quite high in the sky."

And sure enough in the tiny orange disc I could just make out markings which I admit with the aid of the alcohol one could easily believe were artificial. I had looked at Mars often enough through a modern telescope and never seen these lines, although I had heard that early astronomers had theories about Mars canals. And now here they were! But I had also seen the canals drain away underground in the Martian's mind at Helmsley. Proof of the time line we might be on and proof that the Martian vision had been based on truth.

However, a small bell was ringing in the back of my head. A question of too much coincidence was sloshing about. I'm just back from Mars and here I am looking at it again.

"So, James, do you think there are creatures on Mars?"

The bell was getting louder.

"What, you mean are there little green men?"

He looked at me suddenly quite seriously.

"Why do you think they are green?"

"Oh, I read a humorous little story about an invasion by little green men from Mars."

"Did it have a description of them?"

I think the last port was beginning to have an effect on me because for some reason I decided to use the exact description of a Martian.

"The author said they were quite small, about three-foot-high and cat or rabbit like in appearance with a tail like a kangaroo."

"Interesting. Mmh. Like a rabbit you say. And could they fly?"

This was getting a bit scary.

"From what I remember some had wings and they could float in the air."

He turned away from me and looked up at the sky for a moment then said to no one in particular.

"The only ones I've seen are a shade of grey or white. Are you alright, James? You look a little unsteady on your feet. Not used to the port, eh? Perhaps it's time to retire. Shall we return to the ladies?"

--- ~ ---

Chapter Nine

E.

James seemed a little worse for wear and rather pensive and it was with some difficulty I retired him to bed without waking up the whole household from the noise of the squeaking springs. Failing to find a position where any movement did not cause another 'boing' or 'ping' I became convinced that Lilly and her friends had 'fixed' the bed to provide them amusement. If it was then it was well done because I knew if I complained to her the next day I would be on a losing wicket, convincing her that the noise was not caused by a night of 'frolics'. I must record that as well as becoming a criminal thief it is now becoming exceedingly difficult to maintain any pretence of honour or modesty with anyone!

The next morning after a rather fitful and noisy night I dressed and went down for breakfast. James eventually appeared and said:

"I've had a word with a footman about the bed."

"What did you say?"

"I said if I'm going to try and make passionate love to my wife I don't want the whole house listening."

"James!"

"Don't worry I only said "trying" I didn't compromise your honour by saying I succeeded."

"James! Any chance of success in that area is now only in your imagination... "

Before I continued, he said:

"Of course I didn't say that. I gave him a fiver and said I expected it sorted by tonight."

"Five pounds, James? You do realise you have given him over a month's wages?"

"Really? Well I expect a good job then. Now let's have some breakfast. Mmh! Bacon, eggs, sausages and fried bread, perfect!"

How I was going to look the servants in the eye I don't know. And as for Lilly. God knows how it was going to be embellished.

We broke our fast in silence until James said:

"Do you know what your father said last night?"

I saw an opportunity to pay back his teasing.

"Why? Has the port caused you amnesia? I could not begin to recount the failures in etiquette at the table, and as for snatching the last of the port from my father and your rather obvious innuendos regarding Flory's and Freddie's relationship."

"What? I don't remember that! How much did I drink? God, where can I hide? Please forgive me!"

"Touché!"

The look of shock on his face at being 'had' was a picture which I would have recorded for posterity if I had had his phone.

"God, I love you! No other girl keeps me on my toes like you. Anyway back to what I was going to say. Oh yes. Your father and I were discussing what Martians look like."

"So this is what men discuss in their smoking rooms. Is laudanum usually available to assist?"

But James was in earnest and cut to the quick.

"He's seen them, Elizabeth."

I could see he was deadly serious.

"Are you sure it was not the port?"

"No. I mean Yes. Oh you and your negatives. You know what I mean. He described them down to the colour!"

My father in league with the Martians! I made James recount every detail he could remember.

"He gave me the impression he'd been seeing them for years. Hold on, he's coming."

My father exchanged pleasantries and joined us for breakfast. He then leapt straight into the topic.

"James and I were discussing the small folk before bed."

I guarded my reply.

"There are plenty of stories about them in Sussex."

"Yes, there are", said James, "I have a friend Heather Robbins at the University who has made this brilliant map of all the folklore in the county. I've got a copy on my phone..."

I gave James a sharp kick on the shins, but it was too late.

"A 'phone', James? What is that?" said my father.

"Oh, it's erm... a recording device which allows me to copy documents and pictures."

"Do you have it here?"

I kicked him again but not so hard.

"Oh no. Far too big. It's kept in my laboratory."

"Pity. I would have liked to see it."

"So, Father, where can we find these fairies?"

"The usual places. Chanctonbury, Harrow Hill, the Devil's Humps up by West Stoke."

I plunged in.

"And have you seen them, Father?"

"Yes, as I was telling James. Now don't look at me like that, Lizzy. Haven't seen them for a while but Old Eagle Eye and I on our rambles often saw sight of them late in the evening. A little unnerving really. You'd just see them out of the corner of your eye then they'd be gone. Anyway what are you doing today?"

James jumped in. "We haven't decided yet. Maybe we could go and look for your fairies. What do you think, Elizabeth?"

Before I could answer, my father said:

"Why not? It looks like a fine day. I'll get Cook to make up a picnic. Would you like a couple of horses? Wilkinson down at the stable has a couple of good fillies."

James dropped his fork.

"If it is alright with you, sir, I'm not too keen on a horse. They haven't a lot of respect for me."

"Oh, I'd put you down as a horseman. Never mind you can borrow the trap. I'm sure Elizabeth would love to show off her skills."

The day was going to be quite enjoyable after all.

--- ~ ---

J.

I eventually managed to climb into the trap next to Elizabeth who asked:

"And what fairies shall we visit today?"

She had changed into a heavy dark green skirt and jacket with a bonnet closely tied to her head. I had been persuaded to put on a leather jacket and coat which I thought was too warm until we started travelling.

"I had a look at Heather's map and I reckon we should try Harrow Hill. It's only about ten miles if we go via Pulborough. Should be able to do it about an hour and a bit. We can have our picnic there."

"And pray tell me, sir, what would entice a lady there?"

"According to her info it was the last place that fairies lived in England. So that should be where the freshest evidence should be. Also, it's peppered with prehistoric flint mines and I wouldn't be surprised if they've served another purpose."

"Then we must go for I do not want miss meeting with the last fairies. Now are you strapped in properly? I don't want you frightening Nelly."

And before I could ask who Nelly was, she gave the horse a light flick with the reins and I was flung back into the seat. You have to imagine travelling in a two-wheeled wooden box attached by two poles to a horse. The wheels were about five feet high and whirled around at nearly head height. The only brake I could see was a piece of wood which could be pressed against the wheels' rim.

She took us across Coldwaltham to Greatham and then up to Kithurst from where we could see Harrow Hill. That's all I will say about the journey except the occasional embarrassment of having to wave at passers-by while my wife drove and, oh yes, the oncoming coaches which, due to some amazing skills on Elizabeth's part on the narrow roads, we managed to miss each time. Then down the other side with a lot of pressing of the brake until we arrived at a jumble of buildings and outhouses called Northdown Farm.

"How are you, James? Did you enjoy that?"

"Absolutely. Especially the bit up Kithurst Hill with the pony and wheels sliding in the mud and nearly going off the track."

"Yes, I did think that at that point we might have come a cropper." She said giving me the distinct impression that 'coming a cropper' was an everyday occurrence for her.

"Now, I will pay a visit to the farmer to see if I can obtain some fodder for Nelly. Then I suggest we leave her here and take our picnic up to the camp."

By this point she could have anything and I would have done it, as long as we were putting a distance between Nelly and me.

___~___

E.

What a difference a hundred years make. I know I could never drive a car and I am sure James would never understand a horse. I thought he would have difficulty with a woman driving but I was surprised to see he was full of admiration of skills which came naturally to me. It does not occur to him that one sex should be superior to the other. However, when I have asked his opinion on this subject, he always gives the expected answer. And I in turn always remember the limitations of my sex.

It was a pleasant walk up to Harrow Camp. Skylarks twittered above the fields trying to draw us away from their nests and startled by our presence a herd of fallow deer accompanied by a white stag raced away towards Whepham Down. When we arrived at the top we took our picnic of cheese and bread and regarded the great Cissbury fort in the morning mist rising above the sea and, to the north along the edge of the Downs, Chanctonbury Rings with its magical circle of ancient beech trees. I was sad to hear from James that in his time a great storm would destroy most of them.

After luncheon we explored the Camp. James had some knowledge of its structure having visited it before and showed me some of the depressions where the flint had been mined.

As we went over the hill we came across one which was still open. It was about ten feet in diameter. James was surprised as he thought they had all been filled in by natural erosion. I reminded him that Barrow digging was still a popular pastime, and it could have been opened recently by a Sunday party out for amusement.

We peered over the edge. It was dark and quite deep. James could not resist throwing a large flint into it and we counted almost three seconds before we heard the sound of its contact with the bottom of the shaft.

"How deep does it go?" For I could see James was struggling with arithmetic in his head. Then he looked at me quite surprised.

"Check this for me, Elizabeth. A half times thirty-two times three squared. That makes almost one hundred and fifty feet deep!"

I did not know the formula, but I could not disagree with the calculation. We looked at each other, then the hole and then back at each other. James spoke first.

"Before we leap in, so to speak, I think we should go back to that farm and see what they know."

This was a sound idea as it avoided any madness or false bravery. We walked back down the hill. I was pleased to see one of the farm hands was cleaning Nelly. When we arrived at the farm we enquired after the farmer and were directed to a sheep barn.

He was busy dipping an old ewe. They were both caked in white mud and by his looks and movement I would say he had known the farm since it was first built. As we approached him, he put the sheep down and walked over to us. I assume that he enquired as to why we were visiting, with an almost incomprehensible accent and dialect that was obviously not normally used for conversation and told him we were out for a day exploring the legends of the old hill forts of Sussex.

"So you've come up lookin' for Pharisees. Well most folk don't believe in 'em. But they've been mighty busy recently. Holes appear and disappear. And at night sometimes lights be seen up there," pointing at Harrow Camp, "and Chancton."

"Have you been up to see?"

"Best left alone. They don't disturb me and me not them."

"What do you think they are doing?"

"Fairy stuff. That's all. Not of this world and not Godly."

"Do they ever come down here?"

"Not that I'd seen but I'd heard 'em scurrying about. So where be you going now?"

"Over to Chanctonbury."

"Well, watch the green road. It's well rutted from the winter rain."

Chanctonbury was as mysterious as I remembered. The great beech trees shaded the camp darkly. We both felt it and only ventured in a little. As at Harrow there were signs of disturbance in the chalk. After a little exploration we returned the way we had come to the farm. The day had changed. Clouds were gathering in the west over Portsmouth and the Isle of Wight, and the wind was freshening. I sensed rain in the air. By the time we returned to the farm it had arrived.

The farmer took a look at us, my pony and then the weather said:

"Don't fancy your chances to Burpham or Pulborough, Madam. Best you lodge here tonight. Misses'll make you up a bed. It won't be much, but we have good mutton stew if youse want."

James tried to object but the farmer gave him a look and said:

"Youse don't strike me as a man who knows one end of an 'orse from t'other. Best you stay and look after your missus, that's if youse know 'ow to do that."

___~___

J.

The mutton stew more than made up for the derogatory comments about my equestrian skills and Elizabeth was good enough not to remind me of them or whether I was able to 'look after' her.

___~___

E.

I had a troubled and fitful sleep no doubt caused by the wind and squalls of rain on the rafters and window. Strange dreams and revelries came and went. In one James rode a white mare across wild moorland while I chased him in our trap. Each time I drew close I awoke and when I returned to my slumber he once again was far ahead, and I found myself repeating my quest. In another I stood alone while white wraiths flew and fluttered around me and beckoned me to an ancient mound lit by an ethereal glow. I could not resist them and found myself drawn to the hill where a cave appeared into which they tried to entice me. However, as I slowly entered against all my will, I awoke.

It was sitting on the bed post.

Its gossamer like skin was smooth and faintly glowing in the flickering moonlight. I thought or hoped it was yet another dream. I rubbed my eyes, but it remained crouched there motionless. I did not think it had seen me as it seemed to be occupied in regarding the corner of the chamber with great interest. Nevertheless, I felt a cold sweat wash over my body. At first I could not move, frozen by the apparition,

122

but through great effort I moved my arm and nudged James but as usual he was sleeping like a log. I tried harder to no effect, all the while watching for movement in the creature. Then, in desperation, for I needed him awake and calm, I held him where I knew I would have his undivided attention. It had the desired effect. His eyes opened. I put a finger to his lips and by expressions on my face eventually disengaged him and drew him away from what he hoped, to what there was to see at the end of the bed.

We both slowly raised ourselves in the bed. It did not notice us, though now that I could see its form more plainly, it gave the distinct impression it was looking for something. Neither of us wished to speak for fear of disturbing it but I noticed James was slowly reaching for the candle holder by the bed.

Of a sudden its head turned sharply towards us! We involuntarily gripped each other very tight for it gave the awful impression in its crouched position that it was about to leap upon us. James later said that by the strength I held him he was very glad I was not still grasping him in the same place where I had awoken him when I first saw the creature.

We both knew what was coming. We tried to look away but to no avail. As it regarded us the chamber began to shiver and then dissolve to be replaced by that orange world we now knew so well. But as we prepared for yet another involuntary journey it spoke in my head, but they were not words. They were soft impressions of words like the day dreams which flit in and out effortlessly across one's mind on a warm lazy summer's day.

"I cannot hold this future for long. The force is even now pulling me back. I need to freeze time sufficiently so you coalesce into solid apparitions. You slide so easily along time."

The vision blurred and twisted, then snapped sharply clear.

"Ah. Now I can see you and yes, you can see a projection of me."

There was a moment's silence then it continued:

"We have tried to bring you to us. Yes, you thought that was a dream but you were there by the hill when you woke and saw me."

I did not understand how I could be at the hill and in bed. Then more impressions came.

"I now see by your minds that you travel in time. Far farther than us. Let me look. Yes, much of what is to come but shouldn't have been is there. You have arrested all our efforts, yet, yet I see it was not your plan. There is something, something different about you."

A momentary darkness returned, infinitely dark then:

"I have it. You have somehow broken time and are free to travel up and down and across futures, but I cannot understand how this is controlled."

A vision of James and I tumbling through space.

"Nor do you! I can see that. Yes, I can see that is correct. Your actions are dictated by worlds presented to you. I see now that all you want to do is to return to your time."

Another vision. We were at dinner with my father.

"But what time? No, I understand, a time where you can be together. Wait, I am drifting. You are getting fainter. Please, we must meet where you saw us in your dream before sunrise."

My dream came back.

'It is easier for us there. It is where time nodes meet. A place of revelry."

A vision came to me of fairies and wraiths floating in circles above the hill. Then the creature drifted away becoming smaller and fainter until it was gone.

I do not know how I have written this down. I heard no conversation but as I recall it the dream thoughts become words.

James and I looked at each other. The room and wind had returned. If they had ever gone away.

I told James what I had understood. He had seen it too.

"Where was your dream?"

"It was Harrow Camp. It was the shaft or cave, I am sure."

"We must go."

We hurriedly dressed in silence. James brought candles and light, though they were of little use in the wind. Only the rays of the moon showed us the way.

As we climbed the hill the moon raced through the clouds across the sky but did not move. Stars appeared and vanished. The shaft was still there black as night. But as we stood on the edge, we suddenly had a sense of falling or drifting down and down. Phosphorescent strata of flint in the white chalk rose and passed us by until at last we came to the bottom. A soft green glow permeated our surrounds in which stood four of the creatures. Through the dim light they seemed to shimmer as though they had difficulty staying with us. We did not resist them entering into our minds.

--- ~ ---

J.

I had thought they were so light and frail. They were not. It was purely the illusion they gave of trying to stay in our dimensions. What powers were they using to bend time and space?

They were no longer clothed in their gossamer suits. Their skin was hues of shimmering reds and blues and gold. I tried to get closer to see more clearly but a dream appeared in my head which gave words that were not words.

Something or someone told me to be calm and for a moment all my cares and worries fell away from me. I do not know why or how because normally when I visit an ancient hill on a windy night miles from nowhere in a different time to mine and find myself transported down a hole to meet creatures from another planet I get quite agitated.

Then I saw in my mind the fairy folk. They were beautiful small almost dainty creatures. They were as Rolleston had described them in his books of Celtic Legends and as I listened or watched, if those are the right words, I felt as if I was a child who had been returned to his lost land. I became the Irish hero Fionn MacCumhaill and his wife, Sadhbh, my Elizabeth.

I realised that the aliens had come from Mars, not to invade but to share their world with ours. I saw them construct portals encased in stone cairns and covered in pure white chalk, through which we and they could travel between their planet and ours. Then the vision blurred as if hundreds of years passed until once again I saw the cataclysm on Mars. Stars were falling from the sky penetrating the very fabric of their world. Inside their planet, so much smaller than ours, the residual heat from the decaying radioactive core had built up. Instead of releasing its energy little by little, as on our planet along the edges of our tectonic plates, it erupted as bursting bubbles through the surface. The weak gravity made the fissures enormous. I saw the Tharsis volcanoes rise and the great Marina Valley tear across the planet. The beautiful northern seas with their majestic gravity-defying waves disappeared into the gaping chasms until they had all but vanished leaving only an infinite grey swamp from which clouds rose. And in the process I saw space-time become disjointed and they were cut off from Earth.

Then another scene. This time Earth.

Those that were left here lived with the people of our world for a while. But they outlived them and as each wave of newcomers arrived from the east they eventually became regarded as the wicked devils of the new religions and were hunted and persecuted. So they hid themselves in their portals, only seen by those who wanted to see them, the children.

My vision blurred as ages passed until a dark blue sky filled my mind. At first it was empty then out of the blue fantastic space ships slowly materialised and descended to Earth. From them machines emerged and dug great caverns into which the ships were stored or buried. Then another unclear blur as if hundreds of years had passed until the invasion came. The scene vanished and I woke up. We were back on the top of the hill and the shaft had disappeared.

What did this all mean? I noticed the sky in the east was light.

"We must get back before the farmer wakes up. I'm going to have difficulty explaining what we're doing out here."

But as we drove back down the hill Elizabeth said:

"Don't look back but I think we are being followed."

Of course I turned immediately and I swore as I saw momentarily out of the corner of my eye the four creatures floating about ten yards behind us. As I turned back I got another shock. The farmer was waiting by the gate.

--- ~ ---

E.

The sun's red glow spread across the eastern horizon turning the night clouds from grey to pink and orange. I could not see the creatures, but I distinctly felt they had attached themselves to us.

The farmer had a bemused look on his face.

"So you've been visiting the fairies?"

We didn't deny it though I think in hindsight it was a statement rather than a question.

"You ought to be careful. They can get mightily attached to someone who looks for 'em. Don't let go, they don't."

I was beginning to feel what he meant.

As we were not prepared to admit to seeing any 'Pharisees' as he called them, and as he perceived no advantage in pursuing the subject, he graciously invited us in for breakfast. I was pleased to see that James, noticing the poverty of their situation, refused offers of more. He was also quite generous in tipping for the unexpected lodging and stabling of Nelly.

The morning sky was clear, and we arrived rather tired just before midday at Hamgreen. The farmer's comment that 'they don't let go' had haunted me a little on the journey home and I found myself on frequent occasions looking back, expecting to see the creatures hanging onto the trap.

I feared Father would be cross for our not returning the day before but as we partook of the refreshing tea and fruit loaf laid out in the morning room, he was much gratified and relieved to hear that we had been sensible enough to take lodgings rather than risk a journey in the inclement weather.

The rest of the day was spent enjoying the pleasures of home and exchanging tales of adventure with my father.

We retired quite early following an enjoyable dinner after which James had insisted that the cook, much to her embarrassment, should be brought up and thanked for her excellent cooking.

$$---\sim---$$

J.

I don't know whether, after lying in bed with your nearest and dearest having just finished a good book, your thoughts have turned to more interesting and intimate matters. But I have found it is exceedingly difficult to pursue such thoughts to an enjoyable conclusion while four small creatures are sitting on the rail at the end of your bed.

"How long do you think they have been there?" Asked Elizabeth.

"I don't know but knowing my luck possibly just when I finished reading this book."

"Then thankfully we saw them first for I have heard that if a woman is about to conceive it is unlucky to have a fairy present for it might take her child and replace it with a changeling."

"I don't remember saying anything about conceiving, Elizabeth."

"Pray forgive me, James, for I completely misinterpreted the movements of your wandering hand during your reading of the last chapter of your book."

"Ah. I was only trying to keep it warm. Luckily - Ow! That hurt! - I think that the chances of conception in the presence of four fairies at the end of your bed are very slim indeed."

"I cannot but agree, but tell me: Why are we not screaming and running around the room with fear like gibbering gibbons?"

"If you wish to start, I will join you very quickly."

Having decided beyond reason not to follow this path we then turned to the four creatures. They were motionless. We waited for the expected visions, but it did not materialise.

"What do you think they want? They have not harmed us." I said.

"I've no idea; let's ask."

We tried various questions by speaking and also in our heads but to no avail. They just sat there looking not at us but different parts of the room. Every now and then a rainbow hued shimmer went through them.

It was a long night. It wasn't until the first light of the morning brushed the window that they disappeared. We slept until at about eleven we were woken by a gentle knocking at the bedroom door.

--- ~ ---

E.

I was surprised that Lily had left it so long that morning to enquire as to our health and ask if we wished to break our fast.

"Good morning Miss, I mean Madam and Mr Urquhart. Did you have a pleasant night and morning's rest?"

"Yes, eventually, Lilly, for we didn't get to sleep until quite late."

"Well, I am glad to hear it. I would recommend a good breakfast and quiet day to replenish your energies"

By her expression I realised I had not helped myself in defending my honour. This has been commented about by James and his sister many times and is normally accompanied by much mirth and merriment at my expense.

However, James had assessed her character very quickly and came to my rescue.

"Thank you, Lilly. By the way I called on your friend Arnold the footman last night for a snifter and I found he had unaccountably absented himself from his post. You wouldn't know where he might have been?"

Whether there was a relationship between him and Lilly or whether Arnold had actually abandoned his post, I had no idea, but his question was sufficient to immediately bring her under his control.

She replied, rather flustered, "I am sorry, Sir. I will enquire as to his whereabouts and report back to you."

Having got his intended reaction, he finished the chase by saying, a little rudely but effectively:

"Oh, don't worry, Lilly, I expect Nature called. And as you know, Lilly -" giving her a knowing smile, "we must always obey the calls of Nature, mustn't we?"

Considering James had no experience of handling servants this was a marvel which I decided to keep in mind when opportunities in this area were required in future.

--- ~ ---

J.

During the day there was a lot of discussion about our fairy friends and where they were hiding and what they wanted. Eventually a thought came to me.

"Do you think they want to go back to Mars?"

"It is possible but why would they attach themselves to us?"

"Perhaps they discovered at Harrow Camp we had been there and more importantly how we got there."

"So, do you think they want us to return to the cavern at Midhurst?"

"I don't know but it might be the only way we can get rid of them. I'm not quite sure how many more nights I can take with those four creatures sitting on our bed post."

She came close to me. "Nor me, James."

"So, Elizabeth, tomorrow we'll go to Midhurst and see if they follow us."

That night we slept quite well considering the audience at the end of our bed.

$$--- \sim ---$$

E.

We arrived at Midhurst by train, which James preferred. Not knowing where this adventure might lead we bought provisions for luncheon and also four large pies which we were assured had been freshly made and the mutton had been purchased from the abattoir the previous day. Having also obtained two bottles of small beer, which James said were for medicinal purposes, we returned to the cavern via the church. As we entered the crypt the four creatures materialised and followed us down the tunnel. It was quite disconcerting because they became motionless whenever we regarded them.

Marco's Time Machine had disappeared, but all the control consoles were still in place though sadly silent and dead. We knew that of the three doors or portals the middle one was the one Marco and Rolleston had gone through but as we stood there contemplating what to do next, we saw the creatures move and float through the middle door.

The last fairies had left England.

James said "Well, that's got rid of them. Shall we go home?"

"Yes, let us go"

But of course we didn't and instead followed them through the portal after James had very sensibly tested the air with a candle.

We found ourselves on a beach again. But this was different. Gigantic waves slowly rolled across a sea whose horizon seemed no more than a mile away and three small moons hung in the sky. The creatures were nowhere to be seen

I realised we had travelled back to the pre-disaster world of Mars. But how long before? The third moon was low in the sky and travelled at an unnerving speed. Within a few minutes it had disappeared over the horizon.

James had seen it as well.

"I don't think this world has got long, Elizabeth. I can't tell what that moon's orbit is but judging by its eccentricity it's either going to hit one of those other moons or crash here!"

___~___

Chapter Ten

J.

We were on different world millions of miles from Earth and possibly millions of years from our time. Except of course I had come to realise that wherever we were, we were in our own time.

First things first though. Where was the portal we had come through? Elizabeth was already looking. I saw her hand disappear into a rock face and I immediately went up to the place and carved next to it a heart with the letters J and E in it. I thought perhaps if we did not return some future mission from Earth would find it.

As I looked up at the sky the third rock or moon appeared again over the horizon. Had it always been there or had Mars' gravity captured it from the asteroid belt. I turned to the sea. In the distance waves a hundred feet high rose and fell slowly in majestic rows in the weak gravity and washed on to the rocky beach like a slow-motion movie. Then suddenly over the top a white boat appeared and slid down the wave to the land. We watched, waiting, and also keeping a close eye on our escape route. A door slid open, and a familiar figure stepped out and began walking up the beach towards us. He was wearing what seemed to be a translucent sea blue close-fitting tunic. As he got closer it changed colour and blended with the rocks and beach.

"Good afternoon." called out Marco. "Enjoying the view? You'd better hurry up. It's not going to last long."

"Nice suit. I suppose they are still working on trying to camouflage your head" I said trying to keep relaxed. "And what story are you going to fabricate this time?"

"Oh, nothing. Nothing at all. I'm stranded here waiting for the end of time which I think is fairly imminent. So what brings you here?"

I wasn't going to explain anything to him. Instead I replied,

"More to the point, what brings you here? Or more specifically, how do you know we would be here at this time and place?"

"Simple. The Martians told me. Remember they can see the future a little. They saw you coming. Well actually, they didn't see you coming, they saw your four little friends arrive."

Much that I would have liked to stay one jump ahead of Marco I could see unfortunately he was one jump ahead of us again.

Elizabeth said, "So now you're here, Mr Batalia, presuming you did not come visiting just to wish us good day, what are you going to propose?"

"You are not far from the truth. Not to wish you good day, dear lady, but to wish you goodbye!"

This sounded very ominous.

"You mean you want us to return the way we came?"

"Precisely."

"Then what happens?"

"The Martians are going to destroy that moon."

He pointed to the rock which once again was rising above the horizon in its jagged orbit. And as he spoke, I saw dozens of vapour trails rise from the mountains behind us and head towards the moon.

We watched mesmerised as the trails, each with a tiny silver missile, turn towards the moon and chase it across the sky until they were absorbed into it. For a few moments nothing happened. Then the moon turned from grey, white to a misty orange. Plumes of dust rose from the surface spreading outwards into the sky and a great fissure appeared across the moon's surface. Wider and wider it grew until incredibly the moon split in two. All this occurred in perfect silence. We watched fascinated as the pieces slowly fell apart and then to my horror started to fall towards the planet.

I felt Elizabeth grab my hand as she whispered, "What is happening, James?"

Before I could reply Marco shouted,

"Oh my God it's going to hit the planet!"

The broken pieces, which must have been hundreds of miles across, were falling towards us. They moved towards us so slowly that they seemed almost motionless, but I could see they were only going in one direction.

"Run for the portal!"

As we reached it I turned one last time to absorb the beautiful sea and the orange clouds newly formed in the dark blue sky before following Elizabeth through the portal.

--- ~ ---

E.

I thanked all the gods we were safely in the cavern again. We all stood silent and shocked by what we had seen. As usual James was the first to speak. It was a simple question that required a long answer.

"What happened, Marco?"

"The fifth planet which you know as the asteroid belt had collided with its own moon sending millions of shards of rock into the solar system. Most stayed in the belt's orbit but many, too many, were flung out into the solar system. Three were captured by Mars. Many others were lost in the seas of Jupiter which thankfully swept up most of the debris. The

Martians calculated that the orbit of one of the new moons was so unstable that it would eventually collide with the other moons and fall towards Mars, completely destroying it. The only option was to try to destroy the moon, but they knew that the resultant debris would damage the planet irreparably, so they decided to go underground in the hope of rebuilding their civilisation there. This was only going to be a temporary measure though. Their real plan was to move to Earth. They had already established portals here and made contact with the indigenous population. They constructed vast underground caverns on Earth to house their machines and people in preparation for invasion. But something went wrong. When the debris landed on the planet it ruptured the space time links with Earth. Those on the planet were cut off, but unbeknown to them one portal survived."

"Do you mean this place?"

"Yes, but they did not realise it was still possible to make it work."

"Until you idiots found out how to do it and went to Mars?"

Marco ignored that.

"We thought the planet was barren and this portal was just the relic of an ancient, vanished race. But they must have detected our arrival and when we found out how to operate the time controls this must have somehow sent a signal to them which told them a portal was now open."

"And they realised they had access to Earth again. What did they do?"

"It seems while we there they got into our brains and found out what the Weber Institute was trying to do."

"And you didn't detect anything? No visions or anything?"

"No. Except suddenly we had an incredibly clear idea on how to set up ComsMesh and what algorithms to use to manipulate humanity."

"And you didn't suspect a thing. You would think social engineers would know when they are being controlled!"

"They don't communicate like we do. You know that. All we saw was an opportunity to improve our technology. The algorithms worked a dream. The world came under our control. It was the greatest social engineering success in history."

"And we buggered it by shutting down the servers and in the process removed their controls. So they took a risk and invaded Earth anyway."

"No, that was a rising by those whom they had planted on Earth. You've seen their caverns, haven't you? When the servers shut down they lost contact with the Net communications to Mars and thought they were under attack and rose in defence. It was a disaster. All their plans for moving to this planet were destroyed. And now Earth is attacking them!"

"So once again two tribes go to war after completely misinterpreting what the other's intentions were. Do you reckon all life is the same in the Universe? Shoot first and ask questions later?"

"Hey! We didn't know that what was going to happen."

"And nor did they. So what's the current situation, Marco?"

"You know what's happening. We're bombing them!"

"I presume on our past records we'll bomb them until they're completely annihilated or have surrendered."

I realised the conversation was descending into a common form of quarrel I have seen amongst men which invariably leads to a digression from the argument. I call it "which monkey has the biggest stick". When I have used this phrase I have found it quite effective though it causes James much hilarity to which even close questioning has not revealed an answer. Though, having now written down the phrase I can see a possible source of his amusement to which I hope he is not thinking what I think he is thinking!

I have thought on occasion that in Councils of War if a woman or two were present the outcome may have been different though James' reference to Boadicea and a female English prime minister when I have suggested this has weakened my argument a little. Nevertheless, at the risk of seeming like a mother telling off two small boys I needed to bring them back to the problem in hand and so I said quite forcibly: "Will you both stop arguing and put down your sticks?"

To my surprise they actually both stopped and turned to me.

Now I had their attention I needed to hold it so I said the first thought that entered my head.

"Why don't we tell the world government the truth?"

"Why would they believe us?"

"We will bring them some Martians."

"Good idea, except we have just ensured that the last fairies or Martians in England have been escorted off planet."

This was a strong argument, but I was not going to be dissuaded.

"Yes, but the legend refers to England. There may be more in Ireland and Wales."

They both looked at each other then me again. They had dropped their sticks.

James said. "You know, I think you have a point. Let's go to New Grange. That was the centre of Irish legends. If there are any Martians left that will be the place."

Unfortunately I knew that to get there we would have to leave the cavern and from experience we had no idea what year it was going to be when we returned to Midhurst. I think we were all considering this for we had fallen silent for a moment which made us realise that the cavern was not.

"Can you hear that humming sound?"

They both looked around.

"That sounds like the server power supply. But it can't be."

Then Mr Batalia noticed something and said, "Look at this! Next to the Earth globe. There's a small red light."

We immediately went over to the globe. The humming sound was still faint but noticeably louder. At that moment James, who cannot regard a mechanical device without picking it up and attempting to take it apart, or improving its functionality, as he calls it, moved a pointer on the Earth globe.

Suddenly the humming became louder, and a wall of the cavern dissolved to reveal a view of the South Downs.

"My God!" said James, "Has this been working all the time?"

Before I could answer he went around to the back of the machine.

"Just as I thought, the Mars globe is still here. Damn I never thought when we were playing with this the Earth globe might have the same function."

I must admit I had not thought this either but then our minds were on other things. James rushed back to the Earth globe.

"I presume now you are going to treat us to another driving adventure as you did on Mars?"

I could see this idea was already planted firmly in James' mind for he mentioned something about its superiority to what I believe he called 'googling' Earth. I had noticed this word was an important part of his vocabulary and when used was invariably followed by an intense examination of his phone. However, this was not the time to indulge in random exploration.

"James, before you start and send me off on a giddy flight around the world, would it not be best to form an idea of a destination relevant to our predicament?"

He looked a little disappointed. I also noticed Mr Batalia was studiously regarding the desks of consoles. James perked up and said.

"Alright, spoilsport, then we'll go to Newgrange if we can. That Ok with you, Marco?"

James had noticed Mr Batalia 'fiddling' as well.

"Come over here, Marco, and leave those consoles alone or I'll have to consider throwing you back on Mars."

I sensed the monkeys were going to pick up their sticks again and I feared that James did not have the bigger one; I was relieved to see Mr Batalia acquiesce to his request. James grinned.

"Now, we have to get to Newgrange... From what I can remember it's on a bend on the Boyne a few miles north of Dublin. Oh dear, Elizabeth, it looks like I'll have to drive across to it. Whoopee!"

And before I could protest he 'treated' me to another hair-raising flight. We travelled at an impossible speed. The effect was like a wild charabanc for the view seemed to be fixed at a certain height above the surface. As we went up over hills and down into valleys I swear my stomach went in one direction and I the other and caused me on at least two occasions to rather loudly take God's name in vain!

Then across the Severn and into Wales skimming over the Gower and over Pembrokeshire until we were flying at no more than ten feet in the air across the Irish Sea. Then the view turned north and over Dublin until thankfully it slowed and came to rest on the edge of a meandering river surrounded by gentle green hills.

--- ～ ---

J.

It was a long time since I had visited the three great megalithic monuments of Dowth, Knowth and Newgrange on the Brugh na Boyne, all built more than five hundred years before the pyramids. It wasn't obvious where they were at first. When I last saw Newgrange it stood on a gentle grass-covered slope which stretched down to the Boyne, and its great white stone walls, restored by the government, were illuminated by a setting sun.

The Newgrange I saw here was a rough grassy mound surrounded by small fields mainly overgrown with thistle. There was no sign of the great double door entrance.

Our first problem was how to get out of the cavern. As before we found the three hidden doors. Using a candle, we cautiously peered through each. The first led us on to the view we could see from the cavern. The second showed pasture land with no mound and the third I didn't recognise but looked on to a low prehistoric grass fort or enclosure.

Marco wanted to go straight for the mound and not able to come up with any reason, apart from the fact that we didn't trust him farther than we could throw him, we agreed to take the first door.

--- ~ ---

E.

Having recovered from our helter-skelter ride, with virtually no support or sympathy I might add, I now found myself tramping across rain-soaked bog grass with what I can only describe as two young boys who were determined to outdo each other in achieving a wager.

James had speculated that we were not in his time as the mound had not been restored to its former glory. Apparently, he said, I should be looking with great interest at a mound over three hundred feet in diameter bounded by decorated boulders and a wall of white stone topped by a grassy hill. There should also be two great stone portals in front of which should be another great boulder decorated with intricate carvings. None of this description was apparent and my suggestion that perhaps we were at the wrong place was not taken seriously either. No doubt reinforced, I concluded, by a reluctance of the two 'boys' to admit to each other that they could be in error.

But I stand corrected for after inexplicably taking the 'wrong' way round the mound and tramping and tripping through bracken, bramble and scree and returning almost to our starting point we found a large oblong stone lying on its side which, with its decorated whirls and circles, James said confirmed his 'hunch' that we were indeed at the right place. Emboldened by this and to prove his point, James then persuaded us to climb over it and through more of the strangling vegetation as he was now sure that the entrance was behind it. I was seriously considering a bill for the tears and cuts in my embroidery and my ruined gloves. But just as I was considering why I had not left his cursed phone on the grass at Hamgreen when I first saw it we discovered above the boulder covered in brambles a hole which, on removing some of them, revealed itself to be a stone portal.

--- ~ ---

J.

There was no obvious sign in which time period we were in. The state of the tumulus indicated we were before 1880s when it was taken over by the government. Then I remembered a folly had been built using stone from the mound in the mid-nineteenth century. I rushed up the mound and sure enough just a few hundred yards away was the stone folly. That made it between about 1850 and 1880.

I began to hope that we were still in Elizabeth's time. I racked my brain for any Victorian diggers. The only name I could remember was some chap called Burchett who had tried to get access by removing the decorated slab in front and failed. I decided to ask Elizabeth if she knew him. But first I had to put up with a little banter.

"Hello, James. Do you remember me? I'm your wife. You know, the lady you have just taken on a mad jaunt across the Earth followed by bog trotting and brambling. You would not have a spare pair of kid gloves about you for as you can see these are no longer suitable for promenading!"

My apology for neglecting my wife took a little longer than expected to mollify her. However eventually I got an answer after promising to take her shopping in Chichester at the first opportunity at my expense.

"There is a Richard Burchett. I thought you might know of him. He is a minor artist of the Pre-Raphaelite school. All I have heard is that he is a bankrupt. My father told me had read that he gone to Ireland and spent time trying open a burial mound."

"Do you what year that was?"

144

"Why, this year. Sorry, I mean 1873. I don't think he was successful. The stone was too heavy. I believe he employed locals with crowbars."

I ran back down to the decorated slab and there were the marks of the crowbars. Further examination showed that underneath much of the earth had been scraped away.

"Brilliant, Elizabeth. It must be around 1873 which means our clothes are OK."

I then remembered Marco and shook my head at his.......

"Not you though, Marco. You'll have to hide in the bushes if anyone turns up. Meanwhile I think we'll have some grub. Did you bring any food, Marco? No? Oh dear. Well you can watch us."

"James! Much as I have some sympathy with your suggestion we cannot descend to the manners of savages. Let him have some pie."

She was right, of course. I grudgingly gave him half of one of my pies. The beer was for me though. I pointed to a stream where if he was thirsty he could get a drink. However, after noticing a look from Elizabeth and quickly remembering my recent falling from grace I gave him a bottle.

I had just settled down to enjoy some pie when Elizabeth said, "Do you know where our vehicle is? I can't seem to see it."

$$--- \sim ---$$

Chapter Eleven.

E.

What clothing I had left in good repair was quickly ruined by our frantic dashing around looking for our transport. It was only found accidentally when Mr Batalia ran towards a hedge and mysteriously disappeared.

"It's there, James!" I said pointing at the hedge.

"Where?"

"Follow me!"

It took not a little faith to run blindly into a hedge but just when I thought the remnants of my skirts were to be shredded completely, I found myself and James back in the observatory or cavern with Mr Batalia whom I could see was as relieved as we were.

"Thank God for that." Said James. "Right, when we go out again, we must make sure we've got a marker."

And he immediately produced candles from his rucksack.

"See, Elizabeth, I told you one can't have enough candles."

As we left, we placed two adjacent to what we hoped was the entrance portal to the cavern.

I am sure in my earlier life I would have been laid to rest in a bed by now, accompanied by my nurse and smelling salts, for there seemed no end to this adventure.

We climbed through the now beaten path, around the boulder, until we arrived at the portal of the tumulus. James lit one of his candles and looked in.

"It's about a three-foot drop to the floor. Then we should be in the main passage."

I prayed there were no bats residing in there. Though why I should be more worried by bats than Martians or fairies I can only surmise was symptomatic of my disordered state of mind.

I dropped onto the floor with a little ungentlemanly but welcome help. The passage, no more than a few feet wide, was supported by massive stones which in the candlelight displayed in relief dozens of patterned swirls. The floor was damp earth but firm. James insisted Mr Batalia went first then me and James behind. I did not object to this arrangement. We must have walked about thirty yards before the passage opened into a cruciform chamber which in the dim light stretched upwards almost twenty feet.

--- ~ ---

J.

In the flickering shadows cast by the candle I could just see the corbelled roof stretching above in steps. But just as I was immersing myself in this wonderful place Marco broke the spell.

"So whose place was this?" Said Marco.

"It's supposed to be the Palace of Angus Ogg, son of the river goddess Boanna, i.e. the Boyne." I said.

"And where did he come from?"

"This is where it gets interesting. All the legendary races bar one came to Ireland came from other countries. Angus however, was part of the Tuatha de Dannan who were a fairy-like folk who descended in magic clouds from the heavens."

"So you think they were the Martians?"

"They are said to be much smaller, nimbler and lighter than the other races. They founded four cities, each of which had a magic device. One still exists you know."

147

"What?"

"It's the Stone of Destiny from the city of Falias upon which the high kings of Ireland were anointed at Tara. It was brought to Scotland in the sixth century and was known there as the Stone of Scone."

"So where is it now?"

"Underneath the coronation throne in Westminster Abbey."

"What? Where do you get this stuff?"

"Everywhere. Want to know where the altar stone of the Delphi Oracle is? It's behind the back stairs at Castle Howard in Yorkshire."

"How do you know that?"

"It said so on the sign attached to it."

"OK, that's enough. So what are we going do now?"

While entertaining Marco I had been looking at the four chambers or what I thought were chambers. When I brought the candle closer they seemed to be passages that vanished into the dark.

I turned back towards Marco and Elizabeth to point this out but when I saw their faces, I could see they already knew and their expressions told me something was in the tunnel behind me.

--- ~ ---

E.

The Martian stood in the alcove. I swear he was not there a moment before. I looked quickly round and saw there was one in each of the others. We involuntarily moved very close to each other and I felt James grasp my hand. I wondered whether these were the four we had taken back to Mars. This question was answered very quickly for into my mind came visions of our night trip to Harrow Camp and a rather curious image of James and I sitting up in my bed at Hamgreen looking distinctly unnerved.

At first the creatures were completely motionless but then through some trick of light they moved down into the tunnel from which we had arrived. We followed for no other reason that we knew not what else to do. I was just preparing to be man-handled once again and lifted up to the portal when I saw it was open and we could walk straight outside! As we exited I saw it was now dark and the moon was high in the sky. I turned back towards the monument, where to my intense surprise, it was once more the mound exactly as James had described it in his time with its pure white stone walls glistening in the moonlight.

"Are we back when it was built or in your world, James?"

"Judging by the sound of traffic I think we must be at least in my time."

"You are quite correct, Mrs Urquhart".

Behind us stood Professor Rolleston.

"You have helped us enormously to save the peoples of Mars. It might come as a surprise that there are many in Ireland who will welcome the Martians here. After all they are embedded in our folklore."

That was the least of my surprises compared with his sudden materialisation outside the tumuli. Had he come via the observatory? When I asked he replied:

"No, I came with the Martians via this portal which is now operational thanks to you completing the time-space circle."

James, who looked like he was still recovering from the sudden appearance of the professor, asked what he was doing here.

"I am taking them to meet my Society which includes members of our government. Would you like a lift or do you prefer to back via your contraption?"

I looked at James. I was not convinced I could take another adventure in time, let alone skimming over the Earth at breakneck speed. But I knew if I stayed here I would possibly be trapped in James' world. I could see he knew what I was thinking.

"Elizabeth, I'm afraid I can't face another trip in that machine. I know this is difficult for you but I just want to take you back to my little home in Chichester and lead an uneventful life with you."

I had already made up my mind. I had made my decision a long time ago when Mr Batalia brought me through time to James' cottage. I put my hand in his and said,

"We will come with you, Professor Rolleston."

--- ～ ---

Epilogue

J.

We were back in the hothouse world of Chichester by the Sea.

The war with Mars had stopped. Humans were terraforming Mars and Martians were devising methods to trap greenhouse gases on Earth. Both races had come to appreciate how fragile their worlds were and they were supported by Gaia, who appreciated their concern for her world and responded in kind.

The portals remained secret. Whether it was because the Martians could see a little in the future and saw something we could not I have no idea. But at the moment both races are working well together. Whether in the future when the threat of extinction has been removed we can continue like this I have my doubts. There is something wrong with our genes.

Marco decided to go back to the observatory and take his chances. Where he has gone I do not know or care. I have no desire to visit the Cavern at Midhurst anytime soon.

E.

This world, new to both James and I, is a delight. He is back in his beloved university and I have a pleasurable occupation lecturing on, and helping to design, Victorian-themed fashions. We also visit Jill who is married to the love of her life, Sean.

Although there are many great upheavals in the world and massed migrations everyone seems to be united in the belief that we have only two precious worlds and to survive in them we must look after them and each other. I sincerely hope we are in a time line where we can make it together. The fact that the Martians are here, with their ability to glimpse into the future, gives me faith in this.

---~---

The End

Other books by this author

from the
Time Travel Diaries of James Urquhart and Elizabeth
Bicester

Book 1 Out of Time

The first diaries of the humorous and sometimes romantic time travel adventures of James Urquhart, minor science lecturer living in 2015 and Elizabeth Bicester, lady of leisure, whom he stumbles upon at a cricket match at Hamgreen in 1873. Despite their banter regarding each other's manners they manage through incredible feats of illogical deduction and with not a little help from James Maxwell, H. G. Wells, the Martians and some strange time devices, to save the world.

Book 2 A Drift Out of Time

In this volume, they have returned home to find they are not only in an alternative future but a different aspect of themselves. To get back to their world they must travel between Mars and Earth, drifting across time and space, until eventually they reach home and discover who the Martians really are.

Book 3 A House Out of Time

Once again, the intrepid couple have "retired' to a quiet life of ease in an alternative world after helping the Martians save the Earth and their own planet. Unfortunately, Elizabeth thought it would be a good idea to visit her ancestral home at Hamgreen to see what had become of it.

….Such is the curiosity of women.

Book 4 The Space Between Time

In these extracts from the Time Travel Diaries we find the intrepid couple enjoying a peaceful and romantic picnic by the River Rother when a motor launch turns up complete with Mr Wells.

Apparently, a certain Mr Tesla has conducted one of his electro-magnetic experiments which has fractured time and dumped everyone in an alternative world of 1895. The problem is that only a few people have noticed the difference.

Mr Wells wondered if James and Elizabeth would like to help.

Book 5 The Time Palace of Mars

If you are taking your Victorian wife to a car wash for the first time, it's a good idea to explain beforehand that the long blue furry cloths banging on the windows are not aliens trying to abduct her.

This will give you more time to think of a reason why both of you are suddenly transported to a palace on Mars where Time stands still and you're surrounded by twelve strangely magical statues of mythological Gods.

Luckily Mr Puddlewick, a bank teller from Threadneedle Street is on hand to help. Even though he has no idea, after attending a lecture by Mr Tesla in New York on communicating with Mars, why he is there.

All he knows, apart from what is behind the frescos on the walls of the Palace, is that he found a strange device which had a picture of Elizabeth and I with a message "Get Urquhart". So, he pressed the Red Button.

Short Stories

The Webs of Time

Here are short stories from the time travel diaries of James Urquhart, minor scientist, who lived in 2015 and Elizabeth Bicester whom he met at cricket match in 1873.

They are narrated by Professor Rolleston who discovered the original diaries and who spent his life, when not hunting fairies, trying to understand their contents and the reasons for their existence.

Three of the stories, Northern Nights, A Holiday in Cornwall and the Haunted Mill, previously appeared in Three Tales Out of Time.

A Drift Out of Time

About Bruce Macfarlane

Bruce is a retired Health Physicist who lives with his wife on the south coast of England, just a few minutes' walk from the sea. When he's not researching King Arthur, he's out walking on the South Downs with his wife and his friends trying to remember all the names of the flowers and mushrooms his wife has identified.

When it's raining he can be found sometimes in his "shed" as his wife calls it, trying to master new jazz chords.

A life of writing scientific reports and reading early science fiction, especially the genre of time travel such as the works of Anderson, Simak and Wells encouraged him to start writing his own novels about the adventures of a modern man and a Victorian lady whom he met at a cricket match in 1873.

His stories have been described as "Tom Holt meets P.G. Wodehouse meets Philip K. Dick meets Fortean Times."

You can get more information on this and his other books and hobbies at: his blog at:

www.timetraveldiaries.co.uk

Or you can visit our website at:

www.aldwickpublishing.com